SWEET MEAD FOR LADY MARTINE

BELOW THE SALT
BOOK SEVEN

ELIZABETH ROSE

OLIVERHEBERBOOKS

Cover art by Dar Albert at Wicked Smart Designs

Published by Oliver-Heber Books

0 9 8 7 6 5 4 3 2 1

 Created with Vellum

CHAPTER I
DEVON, ENGLAND NOVEMBER, 1375

"Hold on to me, Sage. We'll be out of this weather soon, I promise. Everything is going to be all right, you'll see." Lady Martine Blake sat in the back of the wagon gripping the hands of her pregnant sister-by-marriage who had unexpectedly gone into labor a sennight early. With the girl's back up against the side of the wagon, Sage winced every time one of the wheels of their vehicle hit a rut and almost threw them over the side.

"It's starting to rain," said Josefina, Martine's newest family member who had recently married Martine's cousin, Lord Gar. "I'm afraid to say we're about to get drenched."

Martine glanced upward at the late afternoon sky. Dark clouds covered what little sun there was to begin with, making it a very dreary day. The wind picked up, sending a shiver right through her. Sure enough, what Josefina said was true. The ominous-looking sky started to open and she felt the sting of cold raindrops hitting against her.

"Damn it, what else could go wrong today?" came the

gruff voice of Gar who was on his horse leading their traveling party to Blake Castle. Gar was a big man with long, dark hair. He loved the sea and sailing and had even been raised by pirates as a baby. Gar was the best protector anyone could want. "We never should have attempted this trip. I knew it, but no one would listen to me," he continued to complain to no one in particular. "Josefina is right. We're going to be drenched in a downpour in another few minutes." He raised the hood of his cloak to cover his head.

"Gar, you're not making things any easier," snapped Martine. "Josefina, help me to cover up Sage with this blanket." She pulled her hands away from Sage who was now breathing heavily. The poor girl looked so frightened. Sage reached out to rub her very pregnant belly.

"I feel so helpless," moaned Sage who was a healer by trade. She had been a commoner who married a noble– Martine's brother, Robin. It was becoming a frequent act in Martine's family circle for one to marry from below the salt. And each time it happened, her Uncle Corbett Blake became angry, wanting nothing more than to clear the family name. The more he tried, the worse it got. It was almost funny in a way that two of his own children as well as some of his nephews and nieces married below their status even though at first he fought it. Lord Corbett accepted these pairings eventually, but still had hope for someone to marry wisely. Martine had the feeling as soon as he returned he'd be talking with her father about betrothing her to a noble next.

"You're not helpless. Now, hush," Martine told Sage.

"But I can usually help others with any ailment," Sage continued, really bothered by the fact that she was now the patient instead of the healer. Right now, I can't even help myself."

"No one expects you to. Not in your situation," Martine pointed out, trying to soothe her.

By the contorted twist of Sage's face, Martine was sure the girl was feeling contractions from the baby. That wasn't good because it meant the baby was coming and they weren't ready yet for it to be born.

"I want Robin," cried Sage. "I can't birth this baby without my husband by my side."

Martine let out a sigh. "Sage, you know that's not possible. My brother is serving the king with most of the men of our family right now. We don't even know when they'll return. But we're here with you so there is no need for worry. You are in good hands." Martine hoped to ease the girl's nerves, but her words unfortunately only appeared to do the opposite.

"Nay, nay," wailed Sage, her head thrashing back and forth, bouncing against the side of the wagon as they traveled down the bumpy road. "Robin is going to die in battle, I just know it. He'll die and never even get to see his baby."

"Enough with that kind of talk!" scolded Josefina. "You are stronger than that, Sage. Hush now." Josefina was once the widow of a trade merchant before she married Martine's cousin, Gar. She was also a very independent woman who was never afraid to say what she thought. "You're only going to make this baby come faster with all your fussing." Josefina gripped one end of the blanket while Martine held the other, creating a tent over the pregnant woman so she wouldn't get wet. While it might have given her temporary protection from the rain and cold, it would do nothing to stop the baby from being born early.

"You know Robin would be here if he could," Martine told the distraught woman. "He'll be so excited to return to find out he is a father."

Sage moaned and started to cry. Martine didn't know what to say to help the dire situation. It was already as dark as nighttime with the approaching storm. Lightning flashed in the sky, followed by the sharp crash of thunder, making them all jump. The rain started to fall harder and faster. She wished they'd get to Blake Castle soon so Sage could be in the comfort of a soft bed and able to enjoy a warm fire. The castle's midwife would be there and know what to do. Only then would they have all the help they needed. Then, everything would be all right and they'd have no need to worry.

Their trip from Hythe started over two days ago. They'd been at Saltwood Castle where they were visiting with Martine's cousin Eleanor and her family. Martine's family didn't want Sage staying at her own castle in Shrewsbury while Robin was away and she was so pregnant. They never would have left Saltwood if it hadn't been for the missive that arrived saying Lady Devon, Martine's aunt, had taken ill.

Sage was the family's healer ever since she'd met Robin. It was her choice to leave Saltwood at this time because she decided she wanted to help Lady Devon in Lord Corbett's absence. Sage had talked the rest of their little entourage into making the journey with her. Now, Martine realized she should have insisted Sage stay put until her baby was born.

The traveling party consisted of Ladies Martine, Josefina, and Sage. A teenaged servant boy named Hamlin drove the cart with Sage's handmaid, Lavinia, and Martine's younger sister Regina riding on the bench seat with him. Two armed guards and Lord Gar served as their escorts for protection.

Another flash of lightning split the sky, immediately followed by a loud boom that scared the horse pulling the wagon. The mare reared up, pawing the air. Then the horse started running frantically. The servant boy tried to hold her back, but she raced down the road, out of control. The wagon jerked violently, making Martine believe they were about to be dumped. When they hit the next sloppy rut in the rain-filled road, she heard a cracking noise that sounded like splintering wood. The wagon tilted dangerously to one side causing the women to roll.

"Josefina, help me hold Sage down before we lose her in the road." Martine covered Sage's shaking body with her own. Josefina tried her hardest to hold the blanket over the three of them, but the rain fell harder, soaking them all.

"Whoa! Whoa!" she heard Gar call out, realizing he had turned back to help stop the startled horse from pulling them any farther.

"The wheel is broken, my lord," announced Hamlin. "It will need to be fixed before we're able to continue."

"Then do so," instructed Gar.

"My lord, we left in such a hurry that I'm afraid we don't have the proper tools to repair it."

"Damn it," Gar ground out.

"Stay here with Sage," Martine instructed Josefina, crawling out from under the blanket. "Gar," she shouted to her cousin, hoping to be heard over the raging weather. She raised the hood of her cloak over her head, but the rain continued falling harder and faster than ever. "Gar, Sage is in labor," she shouted from the wagon. "We need to find shelter immediately."

"What?" Gar called over his shoulder, getting off his horse to inspect the damage to the wheel and cursing some more. The handmaid and Regina clung to each other on the front seat of the wagon, shivering in the cold.

"Sage's baby is coming!" yelled Martine. "We need to get her out of the rain anon. She needs a midwife, and quickly."

"God's eyes, I cannot believe our ill luck." Gar looked up, pushing back his long, wet hair.

"How close are we to Blake Castle?" asked Martine, realizing they must be getting nearer since she could see a town or village just up ahead. Usually the lord of the castle gave protection to the commoners of a village or town that was on his land. In return for protection, the commoners paid rent to the lord every month.

"It will take close to a half hour on horseback to get to the castle, mayhap more with this storm to contend with," Gar told her. "We'd have to travel slowly. But it doesn't matter. With this broken wheel, I'm afraid none of us are going anywhere right now."

"Ooooooh, we need to get to Blake Castle," screamed Sage, followed by the sound of her blowing deep breaths from her mouth.

"We need to get her help right now!" Josefina stuck her head out from under the blanket. "I think the baby might be starting to emerge."

"We have to get her indoors and out of this rain." Martine shaded her eyes and took in her surroundings. Through the rain she saw light and buildings in the distance. It was just up the road a bit. "What about there?" she asked Gar, pointing. "Mayhap we can find shelter in that town. Hopefully they'll have a midwife. That would be helpful right about now."

"I don't like the idea of stopping, but I suppose we don't have a choice." Gar jumped up onto the back of the wagon.

"What are you doing?" gasped Martine.

"I'm going to carry her," he explained. "It doesn't sound as if she can walk. And this wagon isn't going to move until the wheel is repaired."

"Good idea. Carry her," said Gar's wife, Josefina, pulling away the blanket and trying to help him with Sage.

"Are you really going to carry her that far?" asked Martine.

"We have no choice. It would be too dangerous to put her on my horse in her condition. We'll stop at the first shelter we see." Gar picked up Sage and her head fell back over his arm as she wailed once again.

"There is an inn up at the crossroads, Lord Gar," one of the guards shouted back to them. "I've visited it on occasion. It's not as bad as most of them."

"That'll have to do," Gar answered. "Declan, ride ahead and secure us lodgings for the night. Dexter, you, and Hamlin gather our things and bring them, the horses, and the women to the inn," he instructed the other guard and servant boy.

Martine picked up a bag and slung it over her shoulder, scooting off the end of the wagon. She followed Gar as he made his way toward the inn.

"Please, by all that is holy, help us," Martine prayed aloud, hoping there was someone at the inn who would assist them. She was frightened right now because Sage could actually lose her baby.

"Dirk, don't let anyone else enter," David Stone, proprietor of the Cross Hare Inn, shouted across the room to his cousin who was guarding the door. "We're too crowded in here. The customers can't even move anymore and there is nowhere for anyone to sit."

"I don't know if I can stop them from coming in," Dirk shouted back. "The storm is picking up and everyone wants to find shelter." Dirk was a big and intimidating man with wide shoulders and a large belly. Just a few years older than David's twenty-three years, Dirk was the muscles of the operation while David liked to think of himself as the brains. Dirk stood every night inside the door to the inn collecting the entry fees of those who entered. It was a small fee of only a farthing but would be used to replace anything possibly broken in a brawl.

Dirk's nearly blind father, Josef, sat in a chair next to the door. It was his job to bounce the coins on a board to make certain they were real. Uncle Joe could tell just by the sound and weight of the coins if someone was trying to cheat them. He had a keen ear since his sight had diminished years ago. More than once now since David's father passed away had Uncle Joe heard trouble before it had a chance to start.

David didn't have enough help to serve all these people. He was glad his business had picked up, but didn't like so much of a crowd all at once. At this rate, they'd run out of food and drinks quickly. The last thing he needed was an angry horde on his hands.

"Where's my ale?" complained a man sitting on a stool at the drink bar. His clothes and hair were totally drenched from the storm.

"I've been waiting longer than you for my whisky," came the complaint of the man next to him who was somewhat dryer but still looked to have been caught in the rain. The men were ornery and most likely cold since there was no room near the hearth to get dry or warm. It was evident that a fight was about to break out.

"Calm down. You'll all get served in time. Just be patient." David quickly poured the drinks and handed them to the men, collecting the coins in return. His pregnant older sister, Cecelia walked out of the kitchen carrying a tray loaded down with bowls of pottage and small loaves of brown bread. "Here," said David, snatching a loaf of bread off the tray and tearing it in half. He handed one piece to each man. "This is no charge for this bread, but only if you both promise not to cause trouble."

David rushed after Cecelia and quickly took the tray from his sister. "You shouldn't be carrying anything heavy," he scolded. "How many times have I told you not to carry trays when you're pregnant?"

"I'm fine, Brother," she said with a swish of her hand through the air. "You worry more than an old alewife at times," she told him. "I'm not due for another two months yet." She rubbed her belly, taking things off the tray he now held and placing the food in front of the hungry travelers.

"David! Help!" came the voice of their younger sister,

Matilda. She was only thirteen but very pretty. Some of the drunken men noticed her and were starting to paw her.

"I am not going to put up with this!" David slid the tray of food onto the table, calling over his shoulder to his cousin. "Dirk, I need you to help me throw some men out of here. They know the rules and yet they continue to try to touch my sister."

"I'm coming." Dirk met David with a few long strides across the floor. Each of them grabbed one of the drunken sots by the front of their tunics, hauling them through the crowd and to the door. David opened the door and pushed out the first man, not realizing a woman was standing outside and was about to enter.

"Awk!" squealed the woman, jumping out of the way of the man flying through the air. Before David could even warn his cousin, Dirk threw the other drunkard outside as well. This time the drunken man hit the woman, sending both of them sprawling across the ground.

"God's eyes, nay," groaned David, seeing the clothes of the wet woman. She was a noble! And as if it weren't bad enough to knock a woman to the ground, this one would probably have his head or at least throw him in prison for what just happened to her. "I'm so sorry." He rushed over and helped the lady up, almost getting trampled by a tall man wearing a long cloak who came up behind her. The man carried a crying and moaning woman in his arms. All the time the rain continued to pelt down upon them.

"Sorry, we're full. No one else can enter." Dirk told the man, blocking the doorway with his bulky body. "You'll have to find another tavern."

10

"But I have a woman in need here. Now get out of my way," growled the man.

"We have no more room," Dirk continued to deny him access.

"She's in pain," cried the woman whom David had just helped to her feet. "We need a dry room and a physician quickly." She pulled away from David and ran to the door, trying to push Dirk out of the way but he wouldn't budge.

"Let them enter, Dirk," instructed David. "Three more people won't matter much. These ones are nobles."

"Nobles?" Dirk's craggy brows raised in surprise and he took a closer look at the newcomers. Oh, I see. All right." He quickly moved aside and held out his arm, motioning for them to enter. As soon as he did, the woman who had fallen earlier entered the inn, clearing the way for the man carrying the woman in need. David wondered what the woman's malady was and hoped it wasn't anything contagious.

"What else can go wrong?" grumbled David. He took a step toward the tavern, but was pushed aside as an armed guard led a procession of people into his tavern that also served as an inn. "Now, wait a minute," he protested, not liking the fact that he, the owner, was just pushed aside.

"We're with them," said one of the women, peeking out at him from under her hood, motioning with her eyes to the people who had already entered his establishment.

That's when David realized there were another three women plus two guards and a servant boy with the traveling party. They all carried large leather bags filled with belongings. One of the guards even had a trunk in his arms. They acted as if they were here to stay, even though his rooms were rented and full. Things were quickly going from bad to worse.

"Where can I stable the horses?" asked the servant boy, holding the reins of four horses that whinnied and pulled, afraid of the storm. The boy's body shook from the cold. "We're also in need of someone to fix a broken wheel on our wagon. We left it down the road."

Standing in the pouring rain, David felt as if he wanted to scream. One problem after another kept stacking up today, only making him regret taking over the inn at his father's demise a year ago.

"Do you have the means to pay for stabling the horses?" David calmly asked the boy, pushing a dripping wet strand of his wavy hair from his eyes.

"Lord Gar holds the money pouch," the boy answered with a shrug. "You'd have to speak to him about it, I suppose."

David's eyes drifted back to the inn. "Lord Gar," he repeated the name, feeling a knot forming in his stomach. "Do you mean the big man who was carrying the woman?"

"Yes, that's him."

"Of course, it is," David said under his breath, letting out a long sigh. There was no use fighting any of this because it wouldn't make a difference. He raised his arm and pointed. "The stable is out back of the inn. You and the guards can stay there for the night but it can get rough with some of the drunken patrons wandering over. Therefore, I don't suggest the women stay out there too. Not unless you and the other men guard them. However, I warn you, I won't be responsible if they get hurt."

"No, no, you don't understand. One of the guards rode

ahead to secure us rooms," the boy tried to explain, looking back, trying to still the horses.

"Well, even so, I'm sure my cousin told him we don't have a single vacant room tonight because that is the truth. This storm has brought every traveler, beggar, and straggler from here to Cornwall to my door this day. Now, go before I change my mind about giving your party shelter."

David walked back into his establishment, glancing around the crowded room, but didn't see the newcomers anywhere.

"They went into the kitchen," his uncle told him from his chair positioned by the door. "I heard Farley yelling at them that they didn't belong in there. That cook is mad. You'd better get in there before he starts swinging his cleaver at them."

"Thanks, Uncle Joe." David hightailed it through the crowd, rushing into the kitchen. He came to an abrupt halt just inside by what he saw. The big man called Lord Gar was about to lay the ailing woman down on the wooden table. The handmaid and another girl hurriedly cleared an area.

"Nay! Don't put her there," shouted David's cook, Farley, waving his meat cleaver in the air. Farley was a small, older man who used to work for the town's baker before his temper got him fired one day. Since he knew how to bake the best bread and David was in need of a cook as well as a baker, he'd hired him. "I prepare food here!" Farley rushed over and slammed the cleaver down into the wooden table, right where Gar was about to place the girl.

"You fool! You almost hit her," spat Gar through gritted teeth. "I'll have you imprisoned for that."

"Nay! This won't solve anything." The woman whom

David had accidentally knocked down outside stepped in front of the man named Lord Gar and held out her arms, keeping the men apart. "Besides, Sage can't birth a baby on such a hard table. We need to find her better accommodations."

"Birth a baby, did you say?" David repeated in surprise. His gaze darted over to the girl in the man's arms. Her cloak had fallen aside and he could now see the large bump at her waist.

"Martine is right," said the other noblewoman. "Gar, we need to find a bed for Sage." They all turned and looked directly at David.

"Nay," he said, shaking his wet head. "I'm sorry, but I am absolutely full. Every one of my rooms is already occupied by at least a half dozen people."

"Certainly you can make room for us." The noblewoman he'd helped to her feet sauntered over, pushing her hood from her head and staring directly into his eyes. He felt his throat tighten just seeing her beauty. He couldn't speak. The girl who seemed no more than nineteen or twenty years of age held her chin high, seeming to have the composure of a much older noblewoman. Her long dark hair was loose, the curly locks falling down nearly to her waist. Smooth and pale skin graced her round face which somehow only reminded him of a pixie. Her lips were full and the color of ripe berries. They turned down into a sultry pout. That intrigued him and only made him wonder how they tasted. This mysterious woman was stirring his loins from just a look.

"Who are you?" he found himself asking softly.

"My name is Lady Martine Blake."

"Blake?" he gasped. "As in Lord Corbett Blake of Blake Castle?" David's town was under the protection of Lord Corbett Blake. He was also whom David paid taxes to each month. David was not on good terms with the man since he was severely behind in his payments and on the verge of losing his inn.

"Yes. Lord Corbett Blake is my uncle," she replied. "His brother, Madoc is my father."

"Wonderful," David mumbled, thinking this was anything but a good omen.

"Martine, Sage is in bad shape," whispered the younger noble girl with her.

"I know, Regina. I am securing a spot for her right now." Martine looked back at David, causing him to feel very uncomfortable being in the middle of this awkward situation.

"You realize, this is a tavern as well as an inn. And right now we are overcrowded," he told the girls. "This is no place for noblewomen and certainly not for one about to give birth. You'd best be off now to find somewhere else to go tonight. The storm will only worsen so you should leave at once." He had hoped to convince them to go, but of course it didn't work.

"Leave? In this bad storm?" asked the girl named Martine, her smile disappearing and her face turning hard now. His words seemed to have made her hazel eyes light on fire. "This woman is in a lot of pain. Her husband is fighting for the king, and we are all nobles. Now find a bed for her at once. Hurry!"

The woman's brash nature caught David by surprise. She had seemed like such a gentle, gullible young woman at first, but not anymore. Now she had taken on the demeanor of a wicked baroness. He stood there with his jaw almost hitting the floor.

"She's right, David." His mother, Greta, wiped her hands on her apron and hurried across the kitchen to join them. "You can't turn them away. They are nobles and in need of our help. We must do what we can to aid them." She turned and spoke to Martine now. "Please, bring the pregnant lady into our private living chamber. Follow me, I'll lead the way."

"Our living chamber? Mother, what are you doing?" David rushed over to his mother, trying his best to make sense of any of this.

"Thank you," he heard Martine say from behind him. "We'll require a midwife as well. I'll pay whatever it costs."

The pregnant girl moaned and wailed and squirmed in the big man's arms as they pushed past David, following his mother to the small room off of the kitchen that was shared by his entire family.

"It's t-time," said the pregnant women that he'd heard them call Sage. "P-please. Hurry."

"Our family's living space is right through here. Just follow me." David's mother opened a door and led the entire procession of people into the small room. Inviting them in had somehow made David feel violated. Never had a noble entered their humble private quarters. It was embarrassing since these people were used to large rooms in a castle. His family's living area held one larger bed shared by his mother and both his sisters. A raised pallet was shared by his cousin Dirk and Uncle Joe. David had his own bed.

Lord Gar put Sage down right on David's bed, making

him want to protest once again. But just as he opened his mouth to speak, the spitfire named Lady Martine walked up to him, staring up at him once again.

"Don't you dare say another word against this," she whispered so the others wouldn't hear her. "My good friend is in a lot of pain and needs help. She is having her baby earlier than she should. This is dangerous and we're not even sure if she or her baby will survive."

"I see," was all he managed to answer, not having realized how dire the situation really was. Now, he felt like a fool for even protesting in the first place.

"We need a midwife. Quickly." Martine ripped off her wet cloak and shoved it into his arms.

"This is an inn, my lady. We have no midwife," explained David, hanging her cloak on a hook on the wall.

"Then go quickly and find one in town," she commanded.

"I can't do that. My inn is busier than it's ever been and I am short on help as it is. I'm not leaving." David knew he shouldn't be speaking this way to nobility, but it angered him that they came in here and basically took over his tavern, his inn, and now even his bed.

"Then send a messenger to do it, I don't care. Just get one," said the girl.

"Messenger?" David shook his head. Did she really think he had one?

"This lady cannot wait for a midwife to arrive," said David's mother, pulling up Sage's gown a little and looking between her legs. "David, call to your sisters. I need them in here immediately to help me."

"Help you?" asked David. "To do what? Cecelia and

Matilda are helping me by serving food and drinks unless you've forgotten."

"We have no midwife and I will need to perform the birth although I've only done it once before. I need their assistance and I need it now," continued his mother.

"They've never done this before, have they?" asked David, wondering how much help his sister would really be.

"Nay, but Cecelia is having a baby of her own in another few months and she needs to see this," said his mother. "I know both of your sisters will be a great asset right now."

"Lady Sage's handmaid can help out in the kitchen," offered Lady Martine. "And if you need help serving drinks or handling the customers, I'll have our guards and servant boy do that."

David noticed that she didn't offer any services from the nobles, but neither would he have accepted if she had. Their status was too high for such menial tasks. He was just a lowly innkeeper and this was his life. He'd probably be flogged if he even suggested that nobles assist anyone from below the salt.

"Someone tell the cook to bring a pot of boiling water and my shears," instructed his mother rolling up her sleeves. "One of you, start ripping up the sheets from the other beds. Quickly."

"Rip up our sheets? Nay, don't do that," said David, getting a death stare from every woman there including his mother.

"Lady Josefina and I will rip up sheets," offered Lady Martine.

The pregnant woman on his bed started to cry and scream at the same time.

"Sage, you'll be fine. Don't worry." Lady Martine ran to her, getting to her knees, taking the woman's hand in hers at the side of the bed.

"It would be best if the men all leave the room now," his mother announced.

"Yes. I agree. Go," Martine told Lord Gar and his henchman, using her hand in a swishing motion to send them away.

"Martine, I'd rather stay in the kitchen than to be here," said the younger noble girl. She looked to be a few years younger than Martine.

"All right," said Martine, putting a hand on the girl's shoulder and glancing over at David. "My sister, Lady Regina, will wait in your kitchen until this is over. She doesn't like to see blood."

"Of course, not. Who does?" asked David with a shrug, wanting to tell Martine that he wasn't going to be happy to see blood either. Especially since the birth was about to happen on his bed.

"You must leave, too," she told David. "Go!"

David didn't like being ordered out of his own chamber. It also bothered him that his pallet would be ruined once the woman gave birth atop it. Still, he didn't protest. He had an inn to run. This was only proving to be a major distraction. He also had to be careful not to do anything more to anger Lord Corbett since he was so far behind with his rent.

"Hurry, David. Get your sisters. The baby will not wait," said his mother with urgency in her voice.

David realized the poor pregnant woman needed help, but on the other hand, so did he. His inn was filled to the brim with drunken, anxious, wet, and angry customers.

These men would most likely start fighting soon if they didn't get the needed attention. He couldn't afford another brawl on his hands. Each time one occurred, the cost of the broken items outweighed the coins his cousin collected at the door.

Releasing a deep breath, David turned and followed the other men out of the room, wondering what the hell just happened.

CHAPTER 2

Martine held one of Sage's hands while Josefina held the other. David's sisters entered the room and closed the door. Martine had never been present at the birth of a child. She wasn't quite sure that she was ready for such an experience. But while she'd told her sister to leave the room, she wasn't going to leave Sage. Sage was a good friend and she needed Martine's support. Not only was she a friend but she was family now. Martine would never abandon family.

"Don't push yet, my lady. Please wait," said Greta, the mother of the proprietor she'd met named David. "I will need those clean pieces of cloth soon. And get my shears ready," the woman told her daughters.

The girls were both very helpful in assisting the woman. They did as told and not once did they flinch. They were strong and as sturdy as rocks. Martine wished she could say the same about herself. All three of these commoners were uncannily calm during this, even with all the crying and screaming in pain from Sage. Martine's nerves shook. She wasn't ready for this and felt dizzy and lightheaded.

"You're doing fine," Martine whispered to Sage, trying to encourage the girl.

"Yes, you are strong, Sage," said Josefina. Sage and Josefina were both originally from below the salt. They were given their titles of being ladies when they married nobles of Martine's family.

"Ooooooh," wailed Sage in pain. "I am a healer and I know something is wrong. I can tell." She gritted her teeth, sweating, and crying from the immense pain. "Tell me what it is. I need to know. Tell me the truth!"

Martine looked over to Greta in question. Greta in turn looked up at her eldest and pregnant daughter.

"Tell her, mother," said Cecelia. "I will be having a baby soon, and I wouldn't want anyone keeping the truth from me."

"The truth? Is something wrong?" Martine had no idea this was the case since none of the women had led her to believe this was anything but a normal birth.

"Mayhap we should have sent someone to town to try to find the midwife after all," said Greta. "I'm sorry, Lady Sage, but I'm pretty sure your baby is breech."

"Breech?" asked Josefina with a gasp.

"Doesn't that mean feet first?" asked Martine.

"Well, I'm not exactly sure if it's the baby's feet or rump, but it sure feels backwards," said Greta, feeling Sage's belly and checking out the situation.

"Can it be born this way?" asked the younger of the daughters.

"It can but it is risky to both the baby as well as the

mother, Matilda," Greta told her daughter, shaking her head. "And I might need to cut her open if the baby gets stuck."

That made Sage scream even louder.

"Nay! Don't do that." Martine thought her hand would break since Sage was gripping it so hard. "There must be another way."

"The baby needs to be turned around," Greta informed her, still feeling Sage's stomach. "It might not be too late to do it, but the baby will need to be guided."

"Well, can you do it?" asked Martine. "Please say yes."

"I will try, but I will need help," said Greta. "It won't be easy. I've never done this before so I'm not even sure if it will be successful."

"Mother, I'm scared," said Matilda, her gaze jutting over to Sage who was squirming in pain. "I don't want to help do this after all."

"Go then," said the girl's mother. "It's all right. You leave too, Cecelia."

"But Mother, you cannot do this alone." Cecelia's voice held extreme concern.

"I don't want you two to be held responsible," said Greta in a soft voice. Fear painted her face.

"What does that mean?" asked Martine.

"She means, if the baby or the baby's mother dies, we will be blamed and executed," explained Cecelia. "This is a noblewoman, not one of the townsfolk. Remember, we are naught but commoners."

"Well, we should send for the midwife then," said Josefina.

"Nay. It's too late," said Greta. "The baby will not wait

and Lady Sage is in too much pain. There is not enough time. We need to do something right now. Besides, there is a storm out there and the midwife might not even be able to make it here because of the weather. We cannot take that chance by waiting."

"Surely, there must be someone who can help you," said Martine.

"How about you?" asked Greta.

"Me?" Martine jerked in surprise. "Nay." She released Sage's hand, shaking her head. "I could never do something like this!"

"Please," begged Sage, tears dripping down her cheeks. "I can tell you what to do as well, Martine. I've done it myself in the past but can't do so now."

"Nay. Of course, you can't." Martine felt her cheeks burning. Her entire body overheated from anxiety and she felt as if she were about to combust. She'd never even been present at the birth of a baby. Now she was expected to partake in a risky process that might end in someone's death? Martine was brave and daring when it came to other things like sailing on a ship filled with men in the midst of a storm at sea, but this frightened her more than even that.

"I trust you, Martine. Please, do this for me." The look of need and hope in Sage's eyes touched Martine's heart. Still, she felt like she didn't want to be a part of this at all. It was much too risky.

"Sage, you don't know what you're asking." Martine couldn't speak above a whisper.

"I, or my baby might die otherwise. Please," Sage continued to beg.

"My mother is putting herself at great risk just to help

your friend," said Cecelia. "She could die for taking this chance but she is putting Lady Sage's needs above even her own protection. Surely, you, a noblewoman have nothing to risk at all by helping."

That was all Martine needed to hear to know that she had to push her fear aside and help her friend. Cecelia was right. The woman's mother was risking everything, possibly even losing her life if Sage or the baby died. Martine didn't want anything to happen to Greta. Neither did she want anything to happen to Sage or the baby. She would never forgive herself if she refused to help and there might have been something she could do to make this a successful birth. Martine cared too much about her friends and family to turn away in their time of need.

"I'll do it," she said, hearing the shaking of her own voice. "I'll do it for you and the baby, Sage. Also for my brother since he cannot be here to aid you. I also don't want anything to happen to Greta when she has been so kind and willing to put her life on the line for us."

"Oh, thank you!" The gratitude in Sage's eyes was enough to give Martine the strength she needed to do this frightening task that she'd never dreamed she'd ever be a part of.

Martine removed the tippets, long sleeves from her gown, so they wouldn't become soiled or get in the way. After releasing a deep breath, she raised her chin and looked over at Greta and Cecelia.

"All right, I'm ready. Tell me what to do."

"Wear this, my lady," said Cecelia tying an apron around her.

"Use this to wash your hands." Matilda hurried over with a basin of water and some soft soap.

"Thank you, girls, but please leave now so you will not be blamed for anything that might happen here tonight," instructed Greta.

"Yes, Mother," said Cecelia taking Matilda's hand and quickly leaving the room. Now, it was only Sage, Josefina, Greta, and Martine left in the chamber.

Martine felt her stomach churning. Sweat beaded on her brow. Was she really going to do this? Could she handle seeing blood or anything else that this might entail? It was absurd! Just the thought of it terrified her and made her want to turn and run. She was a noblewoman and not meant to help birth a baby. But neither was she ready to lose Sage or the unborn child. Today, she would do everything in her power to help Sage or die trying. It didn't matter how she felt about any of this. All that mattered was that this baby would be born healthy and alive and that the child and Sage would both survive.

"Let's do this," she said, holding up her clean hands and releasing one more deep breath, trying to calm her shaking nerves. She pushed from her mind the sound of Sage screaming out in pain, and tried her hardest to stay focused on helping the little, helpless baby.

Even over all the noise of the thunderous storm outside and the talking and the laughing of the people in the crowded room of patrons, David could still hear the screams of the pregnant woman coming from his family's living quarters.

"What's going on back there?" A rugged man already deep in his cups held out his empty tankard, waiting for David to refill it. "Is someone bein' murdered?"

"Nay," said another man, pushing his way through the crowd up to the drink board. His wife was at his side. "It's not a murder. My wife says it's one of those noblewomen. Is she right?"

"Don't worry about it," growled David trying to act nonchalant even though it troubled him more than he was willing to let on.

"David, that sounds like screams of passion," said Cinnamon, the tavern's whore, strutting up behind the drink board with two men following her around, acting as if they were scurvy dogs and she were a bitch in heat.

"You've hired another whore haven't you? How could you?" the girl asked him. "I thought we had a deal that I would be the only whore here at the inn."

"Nay, I didn't hire anyone." David talked over his shoulder as he hurriedly tried to refill the empty cups of the angry men, taking their money, and shoving the coins into the pouch hanging at his side. "I've done no such thing, I swear. I've honored the agreement you made with my father years ago."

"A whore? Oh my!" The patron's wife gasped and held a hand to her mouth. Then she whispered into her husband's ear.

"My wife thinks you've got noble whores here now too. Is that true?" asked the man, getting a slap on his arm and a dirty look from his wife for revealing what she'd told him in confidence.

David glanced back over his shoulder, realizing the

screaming had finally stopped. He wanted more than anything to see what was going on in his chamber, but wouldn't dare leave the drink board. He didn't trust any of these people. It had been a good hour or two now and still no one but his sisters had left the room. He hadn't had even a minute to find them and ask them what was happening with the birth.

"Well? Is it true?" asked the man again.

"Nay, it's not true and I won't tolerate such talk in my tavern." David hoped his answer would stop the tongues from wagging.

As soon as he said the words, the kitchen door opened. The noblewoman named Martine walked out with a dazed look upon her face. Her hair was mussed and she had a strange smear across her cheek. The sleeves of her gown were missing. The lacing on her bodice was loose, exposing the tops of her breasts. A tired expression was mixed with a slight smile on her face.

"Lady Martine," said David. "What happened in there?"

"It was really rough," said the girl, pulling a stray strand of hair from her mouth. "I was frightened at first but decided not to fight it."

"Oh!" gasped the customer's wife again.

"It looks like you enjoyed yourself, Honey." Cinnamon's hands went to her hips.

"It wasn't enjoyable but the results were so satisfying that it made it all worthwhile." Martine's smile turned into a full grin.

"My lady?" asked David, hoping she would explain herself since the whore and patrons were taking this the wrong way.

"David, I'm sorry your bed is ruined but I will buy you a new pallet," said Martine.

"There's a man in there, isn't there?" Cinnamon demanded to know.

"Yes, there is a little man, and he is taking everyone's attention," said Martine. "Let me tell you, he was so worth everything that happened in there, even though at first I wasn't sure about any of it."

The crowd started getting rowdy. David would have to quickly explain matters so they wouldn't think Martine was a whore. But before he could say a word, Martine grabbed on to his arm. He turned to look at her and noticed her eyes rolling back in her head. Her face seemed extremely pale. Then her knees buckled and she fell up against him. He reached out and caught her before she hit the ground, scooping her up into his arms.

"Now you're going to bed her too? Hmmph," snorted Cinnamon, sounding disgusted.

"Out of my way, all of you," he ground out, hurrying into the kitchen with Martine in his arms. She had fainted. Her eyes were closed and her head fell back with her long beautiful tresses hanging nearly to the floor. "Mother!" he shouted, not knowing what to do with the girl. "Mother, where are you?"

His mother opened the door to their living quarters, looking out while she wiped her hands on a towel. "What is it, David? And stop all that shouting. You are being much too loud."

"She fainted. I need to lay her down."

"Oh, no. Lady Martine!" exclaimed his mother.

David pushed past his mother into the room, stopping

when he saw the blood all over his pallet. There was a mess everywhere. Lady Sage sat propped up with her head against the wall and her legs still spread with her gown pushed up to her waist. She held something in her arms.

"David! You cannot come in here," spat his mother as Lady Josefina quickly tossed a blanket over Lady Sage's legs to protect her modesty.

"Was the birth a success?" he asked, walking over to one of the other beds and gently laying Martine down upon it.

"It was," said Sage from his bed. "Thanks to your mother and Lady Martine, my baby boy was born and we are both going to be just fine."

"Really," he said, smiling slightly. Now he understood everything Martine said in the tavern, especially about the little man in the room and how satisfying the results were.

"Mmmph," moaned Martine, her head tossing back and forth on the pillow. "Where am I? What happened?"

"You are a hero," he told her, using part of his sleeve to wipe away the stain of blood on her cheek. "I hear you helped to deliver a baby."

"I did," she said, the smile returning to her face. She looked directly at him with hooded eyes. "I did everything your mother told me to do. It was frightening, I won't lie. And there was blood. Lots of it. I felt so hot and my body was shaking." She grimaced. "So much blood." Her eyes closed and she swallowed deeply.

"Shhh," he said, gently touching the tip of his finger to her lips. The action for some reason sent a delectable shiver right through him. "It's over now. Rest, my lady," he told her. "We will talk more later, I promise."

David got up and headed to the door. His mother ran after him, stopping him from leaving.

"David," she whispered. "We can't let them leave here."

He slowly turned around. "What do you mean?"

"It's storming terribly outside. Lady Sage has just given birth. She cannot be moved until morning. Besides, it's not good to take the newborn out in the rain."

"I see what you mean." His gaze darted back to Lady Martine sprawled out atop the pallet, looking like a bedraggled, dirty, but beautiful angel. "Yes, the noblewomen should stay here tonight along with you and Cecelia and Matilda. I will tell Uncle Joe and Dirk that we'll sleep in the tavern tonight by the fire."

"Nay," said his mother, shaking her head. "I and your sisters cannot stay in the same room as nobles. It's not proper. We are only commoners."

"Yes, you can." Lady Josefina hurried over to them. "You have done wonders and saved both Lady Sage and her baby. We want you to stay here with us tonight. Please. You and your daughters as well are welcome."

"Yes, I agree," Sage chimed in from the bed, smiling and rocking her baby in her arms as the infant started crying. "We would have it no other way. I want to thank each and every one of you because without your help there is a good chance that I and my baby would no longer be here."

"Oh, but Lady Martine is the one you should be thanking," said Greta. "She was so helpful and brave. I couldn't have done it without her."

"Did I hear someone mention my name?" Martine pushed up on the bed, looking drained of energy and very sleepy. Her bodice hung open, exposing too much skin. As much as David liked what he saw, he forced himself to look away as was proper.

"I'll make certain no men enter here tonight," he told the women.

"Thank you," said Lady Sage.

"What about Lord Gar?" asked David. "Do I need to kick out paying customers to give him a room upstairs?"

"My husband would pay double I'm sure, but I don't want you to have to ask anyone to leave," said Josefina. "I will talk to him, but I assure you my husband will be fine staying the night in the tavern."

"But he is a noble. By rights, he should have a room upstairs," said David, not wanting to anger a noble, even though he wasn't anxious to kick out the commoners who had already paid for the room for the night.

"I'll speak to him so you don't have to worry," Josefina told him with a smile.

"I need to finish cleaning up and see to the baby now," said Greta. "How are things out in the tavern, David? Are there any problems?"

David opened his mouth, meaning to tell them how the patrons thought Martine was a noble whore, but decided not to say anything after all. It wouldn't be right. Plus, Lady Martine had gone through so much tonight that she didn't need to hear such idle gossip.

"There are no problems that I can't handle," he said, flashing a quick smile. "I'll tell Cecelia and Matilda to bring the noble ladies some food and drink. Let me know if there is anything needed for the baby." David turned to leave, stopping with his hand on the door when he heard the angel's sweet voice from the bed.

"Thank you, David. I remember fainting out there and I am guessing it was you who caught me and brought me in here, lying me so protectively on the bed."

"Well, yes," he said, clearing his throat, feeling like he had done it out of need since she fainted in his arms. Still, if she wanted to think of him as a protector, then so be it.

"That was so kind of you."

David peeked back over his shoulder, not wanting to turn around completely because the smooth skin of the tops of her breasts and that sultry smile and her hooded eyes only made him feel lusty. He had no right feeling this way. He was only an innkeeper and she was a lady from the castle.

"Of course, Lady Martine," he said, looking at the door when he spoke. "I am happy to assist in any way possible." He was about to leave and thought he'd say one more thing since she was in such a grateful mood. "Please mention this to your uncle, Lord Corbett Blake, as well." Lord Corbett had been generous these past few months but David had been warned. If he couldn't pay up all the rent he owed, Lord Corbett would be taking drastic measures the next time.

With that, David left the room and closed the door behind him.

CHAPTER 3

Martine was up early the next morning before the sun even rose. She found herself unable to sleep much at all. One of the reasons was that the baby woke up several times during the night crying. She'd volunteered to rock him and walk with the newborn after Sage had fed him since she knew what a hard time her good friend had birthing the baby. Sage needed her sleep. Besides, Martine liked babies and hoped to someday have children of her own.

"You are cuter than I thought you'd be," she whispered, giving the baby a kiss on the forehead. His eyes closed and he made sucking motions with his mouth in his sleep. Martine gently laid the child down next to his mother and tiptoed to the door. She had changed last night into a fresh gown she'd had in her travel bag. Already dressed and up for the day, Martine decided to wander out into the tavern area since she was feeling parched and thirsty.

Last night she did something that she didn't think she

ever could. She'd helped Greta and together they managed to bring Sage's baby into the world unharmed. Thankfully, even Sage had survived and would recover.

Softly opening the door, she hoped not to wake anyone. What she needed was time alone. While grateful to have a place to sleep, this room in the family's living quarters was small and stuffy. Martine was used to the large rooms of a castle and really wanted to stretch her legs. Making her way through the kitchen, she saw the dying embers on the cooking hearth heating a cauldron that most likely contained hot water used by the commoners to wash up at night.

Through the darkness she spotted light from the tavern, over by the drink board. For as crowded as the place was last night, to her surprise, the tavern wasn't in a huge upheaval. She'd seen some establishments so filthy and smelly that it sickened her even to enter. Here at the Cross Hare Inn it still smelled a little like urine and stale ale but mayhap that was because there were no rushes at all on the wooden floor. It actually looked as if the floor was swept daily. Bunches of dried herbs hung from the rafters, releasing spicy scents in the air.

It was a cozy establishment meant to help the commoners relax. Or at least that is what she thought. She continued moving forward toward the light. There were chains attached to the ceiling in several places, holding up round metal hoops that held half a dozen taper candles. The candles were long and slim and looked to be made of wax. Such an extravagance for commoners to have wax candles. Usually only the nobility or clergy had these. Commoners didn't usually have anything but tallow candles made from animal fat. Mayhap David Stone was different from most innkeepers with his values. Or perhaps he just made silly decisions, paying for things not meant for simple people such as the ones who had been occupying this place last night.

She noticed a few men lying on the floor sleeping. The sound of snoring filled the air. Careful to step over them, she made her way to the drink board where the beverages would be stored beneath. Once there, she bent over and fumbled with the bottles, trying to find what she was looking for. She reached out and grabbed a bottle, trying to hold it up to see its contents.

"Is there something I can get you, my lady?" came a male voice from across the room.

In surprise, she spun around. The bottle crashed to the floor but thankfully didn't break. A few groans filled the air from the men sleeping who complained of the noise.

"Who's there?" she asked, her eyes settling on a man in the shadows sitting atop one of the wooden tables with his legs crossed. He wore a forest green sleeveless vest, like a surcoat over a long-sleeved tan tunic with baggy sleeves. His trews were dark and his soft leather boots went all the way up to his knees. It was the proprietor she'd met last night. The handsome man with the dark brown hair and the sculpted face that seemed much too comely for a man of his position. She remembered looking into his eyes and being drawn in for some reason. He appeared to be not much older than her twenty years. Still, his concerned eyes had seemed to hold worries that were usually only found on a more seasoned man. "Proprietor Stone? Is that you?" she called out in a soft voice, not wanting to wake the others still sleeping.

"Please," he said, pushing a wavy lock of hair from his eyes and stifling a yawn. "Call me, David." In one motion he'd uncrossed his legs and jumped from the table, padding over the floor toward her. "Are you perhaps looking for a drink, my lady?"

He slid behind the drink board and sidled up close behind her. It was a small area and mayhap that was the reason for his body nearly touching hers. Or was it? Being a lady, she should demand that he step away and stand on the other side of the drink board, but she didn't. Being curious about this man named David Stone and his nature, she decided to say nothing and see what would transpire.

"Yes, I'm thirsty. My throat is parched and I didn't want to wake anyone. In the dark, I just wasn't sure of the contents of these bottles." She bent down to pick up the one she dropped. He hunkered down next to her to get it. His hand reached out for the bottle at the same time, his fingers clasping around hers as they both tried to pick it up.

"Oh!" Martine felt the heat of his skin against hers and it immediately warmed her entire being. Frightened of this unfamiliar reaction she was having to a man, she quickly pulled her hand away. Still bent over, she turned her face to look at him. Now, their faces were so close that they were almost touching. The scant light from the candles hanging from the iron ceiling fixture encompassed his face in warm tones. His eyes reflected the fire which almost seemed to make them glow. He looked sensual, she decided. Like a man who wanted to take a woman to bed. Or was it just that he felt tired? Perhaps he missed his bed since Sage was still in it. Either way, she found herself intrigued by him and decided she needed to take this opportunity to learn more about the man.

"Allow me," he told her, taking the bottle and standing up. His hand shot out and his long fingers clasped around her arm to assist her in standing.

Martine's attention shot over to this commoner once again. He was touching her on her upper arm, quite close to her breasts. Was he doing that purposely to get a rise out of her or was it all innocent? She couldn't be sure.

"David Stone, that is not necessary and neither is it appropriate," she told him, only because she was a noble and she needed to remind him not to act so familiar around her.

"I assure you, my lady, it is quite necessary since I cannot be certain you won't swoon in my arms again the way you did last night."

"Swoon? I didn't swoon," she retorted, hearing him snort in response.

"Well, then what would you call it when your knees gave way and you fell into my arms like a willing lover?" He released her arm.

"Stop it," she said softly, feeling rattled by his words. True, she had fainted but it was because of her harrowing experience helping to birth a baby. It had nothing at all to do with her being infatuated by him. She wrapped her arms around herself in a form of closing herself off to him, and looked the other way. Did he really have to say swoon? And lover? That made it even worse. It made her feel so vulnerable, helpless, and dirty. "You cannot speak to me the same way you do to your tavern whore," she spoke her thoughts aloud.

"I assure you, I say no such things to Cinnamon."

"Cinnamon?" Her eyes rose in question, wondering why he was talking about an exotic spice. When he didn't answer, she realized that was the whore's name. "Oh, Cinnamon," she said, her gaze falling.

"Neither did I mean to show you anything but respect, my lady. I swear that is the truth." He made a cross over his heart with his finger. It was a silly gesture but caused her to smile. It made him seem more approachable, she supposed. She didn't know any other man who would promise he spoke the truth and follow up his words by making a cross over his heart. It was almost adorable in a way. She liked that.

"I believe you," she told him, easing up with her accusations.

He reached under the drink board and grabbed a wooden cup, pouring her liquid from the bottle and handing the vessel to her. "Is this what you wanted?"

"I don't know. What is it?" Her arms stayed wrapped around her waist while her gaze lowered to the cup in his hand.

"It's whisky, my lady. It is most sought after by the men who drink here."

"Whisky?" She contemplated taking a sip since her nerves were still severely shaken from the storm last night, as well as everything she'd been through with helping to birth the baby.

"Mmm-hmm." He nodded. Then his tongue shot out to lick his top lip, making her heart jump into her throat since she'd been looking at his mouth when he did it. She quickly averted her gaze, hoping he hadn't noticed. "Perhaps you've had it before?"

"Of course, I have tasted whisky, but it is hardly the drink of a lady," she explained. "You don't really expect me to partake of it, do you? After all, I am a noblewoman."

"Ah, I see. I suppose not. My mistake." He shrugged and downed the whisky, inhaling a sharp breath and then releasing it slowly. A satisfied grin spread across his face. "However, you don't know what you're missing." He put the bottle and the cup on the drink board.

"I don't care to know, thank you." She swore his face got redder just from that one drink of the potent liquid.

"It's quite relaxing. You really should try it."

"It's not ladylike," she said again, eyeing up the cup and almost wanting the whisky after all.

He leaned over with one elbow on the drink board, smiling up at her, speaking in a whisper. "I'll bet there is a lot about you that isn't so ladylike. Am I right?" His eyes twinkled with mischief when he said it.

"I'm sure I don't know what you mean."

"I think you do." He slowly stood up and reached out to cup her chin in his hand, causing her heart to beat rapidly. "I heard you recently took a journey aboard a ship filled with questionable men." He moved even closer and cupped the back of her head with his other large palm. Her eyes closed. He was going to kiss her! She just knew he was. Why wasn't she stopping him? Mayhap because she wanted him to kiss her and hadn't been able to stop thinking about it all night? He was right. That wasn't ladylike at all, but neither did she care.

"Yes, I did that," she whispered, raising her chin with her eyes still closed as she prepared herself for his kiss. "A ship filled with men."

"You've got dried rosemary in your hair." He plucked something from her hair and her eyes sprang open to see him throwing it to the ground. He quickly turned and studied the bottles lined up on a shelf behind the drink board.

"Oh. Thank you," she whispered, feeling foolish for her illicit thoughts. She ran her hand over her hair, trying to still her rapidly beating heart. "I must have brushed up against some of the hanging herbs when I walked out here through the kitchen."

"Ah, here we go. This is the drink of a lady." He plucked up another bottle and brought it over to the same wooden cup he'd just drank from, pouring some into it and holding it out to her. "It's a woodsy red wine with a hint of spices that I had my cook infuse into the liquid."

"Oh, so it's not mead? I love mead. The sweeter the better." She knew by the scowl on his face that it was not.

"Nay, of course it isn't mead. This is a tavern, my lady. We don't serve mead here."

"Why not? You should serve it. After all, you never know when someone might want some."

"I doubt anyone ever would. Most of my patrons are rugged men. I assure you, none of them want a drink like sweet mead. It would be downright embarrassing. After all, that is a drink for a lady."

"Oh, so now I'm a lady again, am I?" She boldly pointed out the fact that he'd just accused her of not being very lady-like but now he had suddenly changed his mind.

"Of course, you're a lady. My lady," he added, his mood changing as fast as the unpredictable weather. His friendly, playful smile faded. "I only point out to you what is available at the Cross Hare Inn. And it isn't sweet mead, I assure you. If you want that, I suggest taking a journey to Blake Castle where I am sure they will cater to all your wants and needs."

She'd been enjoying talking with the man, but she had somehow soured the mood between them asking for a drink that he didn't have. Martine found herself wondering if he was disgusted by her request for mead or perhaps embarrassed that he didn't have it. Either way, it no longer mattered she supposed. What was done was done.

He started to put the cup of wine down on the drink board but she snatched it away from him and drank it down in three gulps, her eyes never leaving his.

"You weren't jesting." He cleared his throat. "You really were thirsty."

"Birthing babies and swooning at the feet of common innkeepers takes a lot of energy, you realize. Plus, it makes one very thirsty." She pushed past him, meaning to go back to the small, stuffy room with the other women.

"Please stay," came his request from behind her, making her stop in her tracks.

"Stay?" she asked, slowly turning around. "Why? So you can insult me again?"

"Nay, of course not." He shook his head and held up one palm. "I'm sorry if you think that way, because it was not my intention at all to insult you, Lady Martine. I acted a little too familiar with you I suppose, but I was only enjoying being with you. Talking with you, I mean. Not being with you. Not in an improper manner." He looked as if he could kick himself, thinking he'd said something wrong.

Martine liked it when David used her Christian name. It sounded good coming from his mouth. Now she found herself wanting to hear him say her name once again. Mayhap the best way to promote it was to use his Christian name as well. "I forgive you. David," she said, liking the way his name sounded on her tongue. "I must admit that I had been enjoying talking with you as well."

"I'd like to get to know you better," he blurted out. His eyes popped open and he looked horrified by what he'd said. "Not know you. I mean, not like that. Not what you think."

"And what do I think?" she asked playfully, being the mischievous one now.

"What I mean... what I meant–"

"I know what you meant, David," she said with a smile, trying to make him feel relaxed. "Now, if you'll pour me some more of that spiced wine, mayhap we can sit down at that empty table together and continue talking." She nodded with her head to the same table he'd been sitting on when she walked in. The one in the shadows at the back of the room. She realized now, he must have been sleeping atop it since Lady Sage and her baby were in his bed.

Martine headed to the table. David was right behind her with a wooden cup in his hands and a corked bottle tucked under his arm. She sat down on the bench. He settled himself across from her. Putting the cup on the table, he filled it to the brim and handed it to her.

. . .

David felt more than uncomfortable sitting down with Lady Martine and drinking wine in the semi-darkness. He felt as if he were sneaking around and doing something forbidden. But she was the one to suggest it and he wasn't about to deny her wishes. Especially when they were really his wishes too.

"Here you are, my lady." He handed the cup to her, but she hesitated to take it. The look on her face made him wonder if she was regretting his presence after all. Or mayhap the wine wasn't good enough for her. Oh, why the hell didn't he have sweet mead in his tavern? But why should he when she was the only one who had ever requested it? Worried thoughts filled his head and made him wonder if she was just testing him somehow. Perhaps she felt as if she were too good to be sitting with him. After all, he was just a commoner. These thoughts almost made him angry. "Take it, my lady. Or should I have brought you your wine in a chalice instead?"

"A chalice?" One of her thin brows raised and she looked at him from the corner of her eye.

"I meant, goblet. Goblet, not a chalice," he hurriedly corrected himself. Damn, why did he feel so vulnerable and insecure around her? Mayhap he should have poured more whisky for himself so he could rid his mind of his own thoughts of pity. After all, she was a noble from the castle. Ladies didn't sit down and drink with the likes of him. What the hell was he doing?

"Just relax, David. I only hesitated because there is only one cup. However, I suppose we can share it." Reaching out, she took the cup from him, seeming as if she were being extra careful not to touch his hand. Still, her fingers brushed up against his slightly, and once again excitement rushed through him. She was such a beautiful woman. And forbidden to commoners like him, he silently reminded himself. While he enjoyed when their hands brushed together, she most likely despised it. Why wouldn't she? He pulled back his hand, resting it on his lap, glancing down and wondering if his fingers were dirty. He wiped his palm on his trews, mainly to get rid of the sweat on his palm.

"What are you doing?" she asked, dragging him from his thoughts.

His heart jumped into his throat once again. "I was just... wiping off my hand," he said, not knowing how else to answer.

"You were?" Her smile turned into a frown. "Why?"

God's eyes, had he accidentally insulted her again? Mayhap she thought it was he who didn't want to touch her and not the other way around. Holy hell, why did he keep doing this?

"My lady, it is not right for me to be sitting here with you. What will the other nobles say?" He glanced over his shoulder to where Lord Gar and his henchmen slept by the fire. "I'll leave at once." He got to his feet.

"You're right." She drank down the wine quickly and stood as well. "This will never do. If my brother-by-marriage awakes, he'll have your head for drinking wine with me and having conversation."

"He will?" This only made him feel worse than he already did.

"We'll have to go outside where we'll be alone and also be sure not to wake anyone. Mayhap the stables would be a better choice since I don't think the horses will care." She turned and marched for the door. "Bring the wine."

"Oh, hell," David mumbled under his breath. The stables were the last place he wanted to be caught alone with a noblewoman in the dark. He couldn't go there. Then again, she had already opened the door and wasn't turning back. If he let her leave the inn without an escort, he was sure Lord Gar would truly have his head. "Wait," he whispered, grabbing the bottle of wine and hurrying after her, taking his cloak from a hook on the wall. Just as he was about to close the door, Uncle Joe sat up in the dark, his head moving back and forth.

"Who goes there?" asked Joe.

"Shhh, it's just me, Uncle Joe. Go back to sleep," he answered.

"David? Is that you? Who is with you?" asked the blind man. "I heard two people."

"Nay, it's just me. Now, go back to sleep. Everything is fine." He quickly closed the door and turned to take a step, knocking right into Martine.

"Oh!" she cried out, losing her balance from the force of their bodies hitting against each other. Once again, he found himself holding Lady Martine, keeping her from falling.

"We've got to stop doing this," he said playfully, watching her eyes roam upward, stopping at his mouth.

"Doing what? We're not doing anything. Yet," she whispered, her eyes still fastened on his lips.

He was about to release her when to his surprise, she reached up and pressed her lips against his quickly. Too much in shock to stop her, he let it happen. The bottle of wine almost slipped from his fingers since he was so surprised by her action. And when she continued to stare at him instead of turning away, he lost all common sense. Feeling as if his head were filled with straw, he foolishly pulled her closer and kissed her passionately, not able to stop himself from wanting to taste her essence. His desire soon turned to wanting to taste her on his tongue as well as his lips. Before he could think about the consequences, his tongue entered her mouth. He filled her completely, fantasizing that it was another part of him doing this but somewhere else on her enticing body.

God's teeth, she was breathtaking and tasted sweet like honey. Or mead. The scent of rosewater drifted from her hair, filling his senses, about driving him mad. He wanted her. Badly. His hand went around the back of her head, steadying her while he kissed her even deeper. Her hair was silky to the touch. Her face being pressed up against his made him realize the skin of nobles was soft like the petals of a rose. Or at least hers was. Damn, this woman was even more intoxicating than an entire bottle of whisky.

"Let's go over here," he told her, leading the way to a side of the tavern that had no windows. It was where he chopped wood for the fire.

"We can sit on these stumps and talk," she said, starting to sit even before he could object because it was dirty and wet from the rain. Still, she didn't seem to care.

"Wait, allow me." He put his cloak over the stump. Then he held out his arm and let her take it to steady herself while sitting.

"What did you want to talk about?" he asked, sitting on the stump next to her. The sun was just starting to rise on the horizon taking away the inky darkness of night.

"How about some more wine?" she asked.

"Of course." He picked up the bottle and realized his mistake. "I left the cup inside. I can go get it." He was about to leave when her hand shot out and she took the bottle from him.

"No need. I'm totally capable of drinking right from the bottle."

His eyes opened wide as she lifted the bottle to her lips, swallowing down some wine. His eyes focused on her sleek neck as she swallowed. Martine was one noblewoman who never ceased to surprise him.

"Your turn," she said, holding out the bottle.

"You've got a drop on your lips." He reached out to wipe it away with his finger, but the lusty look in her eyes gave him the courage to do something else instead. He leaned over and used his mouth and tongue to lick away the drop of wine.

She moaned and her eyes closed slightly. Putting down the bottle, he reached out and took her hands. "I want you closer," he whispered, pulling her toward him and she didn't object.

He took her onto his lap, wrapping his arms protectively around her. She put her arm around his neck and leaned down to kiss him once again.

David liked this too much. If they kept on kissing, he wasn't sure he'd be able to stop himself from doing more.

"I scare you. Don't I?" she asked, her face still close to his.

"More than you know." His gaze dropped when he realized her cleavage was right in front of his mouth since she was sitting on his lap. "I'm afraid we'd better separate, my lady. If not, I am going to want to bury my face in your cleavage. God's eyes, did I really just say that aloud?"

She giggled, breaking the tension between them.

"I have never known a man like you before." She smoothed back a lock of his hair behind his ear. An innocent act he supposed, but it felt endearing.

"I have to say I've never known a noblewoman like you either."

"In a good way? Or bad?" she asked.

"I wouldn't think you had to ask, my lady. After all, we are touching and kissing. To me, that is a good thing."

"I agree. I think it's a good thing as well."

"You were very brave to help birth your sister-by-marriage's baby," he told her, liking the way her rounded bottom warmed his lap.

"The baby was breech and I had to help your mother to turn it."

"Oh, she didn't tell me that. I have never heard of a noblewoman birthing a baby before."

"You probably won't ever again." She giggled again, her laugh reminding him of the twitter of a small bird. "Or at least I won't be in a hurry to do it again. Unless it was really necessary, I should say."

He picked up her hand from her lap, stroking his thumb across the top of it. "You have such soft skin."

"You have soft lips. That surprised me."

"Really?" He picked up her hand and gently kissed it, his eyes never leaving her face.

"Yes. I thought all innkeepers were smelly and old and had leathery skin and lips."

"Now, now, that is such an inaccurate accusation to make." He chuckled at her words.

"Well, I didn't know better. Not until now. I mean, didn't you think nobles were... I don't know. Haughty?"

"Aren't they?" he asked, making her frown.

"What?"

"Except for you, my lady. You are the exception." He gently tapped her lips with the tip of his finger. She opened her mouth and pulled his finger in, using her lush lips and tongue to suck on it, about driving him out of his mind. "I think we'd better go." He jumped to his feet and put her feet on the ground.

"I'm sorry. That was inappropriate," she told him. "I'm not sure why I did it, but I can tell you didn't like it."

"Mmm" he moaned, drinking her in with his eyes. "If only you could read my mind, you'd know that what I was thinking when you did that was far from appropriate for a lady like you."

She looked confused. "What do you mean? What were you imagining in your head?"

"You don't want to know."

"Oh, but I do." Her fingers trailed down his arm. This woman was either very playful or a big tease.

"I was imagining something that only whores do for a man, but something that a man thoroughly enjoys."

"A whore?" She looked hurt.

"I'm not saying you're a whore. God's breath, that wasn't at all what I meant."

"I hope you don't think that, David. I'm sorry if I've been a bit too playful and given you the wrong impression. I guess I'm just ready for a relationship with a man after having watched most of my family marry lately."

"Have you had many? Relationships? With men."

"No," she said, shocking him even further since she seemed experienced. "I don't usually act this way around men, but I feel so comfortable around you that I'm afraid I got carried away. Forgive me." She pouted and looked away.

"There is nothing at all to forgive, my lady. Now please, don't turn away." He took her hands in his.

"I like you, David. A lot. But I'm afraid I've made a fool of myself."

"Nay, nay you didn't. I like you a lot, too. I am only pulling back because I might do something we'd both regret."

"I could never regret doing anything with you."

"I don't regret anything we've done so far." He stroked her cheek and was about to kiss her again when he heard someone shouting.

"David? David, are you out here? Who are you with and what are you doing out here in the near dark?"

The sound of his cousin, Dirk, from the tavern brought him back to his senses. He pulled away, his head snapping around to see the big lunk standing in the doorway rubbing his eyes. "My father said you left here with someone. David? Are you out here?"

"Go back to sleep. Everything's fine," he called out. When he turned back to Martine, she was gone. He looked up to see her holding up the hem of her skirt and running across the road instead of heading back to the tavern or even toward the stables. He groaned. "Damn it, you're going to get me killed," he mumbled, grabbing his cloak, and taking off at a dash after her. He knew the area better than she, and had to stop her because there was a creek up ahead. In the semi-darkness, she was going to end up in the water if she wasn't careful. "Lady Martine, wait! Please, stop. You're going to get hurt."

"Just go back to the inn and leave me be," came her command. If he wasn't mistaken, her voice trembled.

"I'll not leave you be. I feel responsible for your safety. Now, stop running away from me or you're going to end up in the—"

Too late. He heard the splash and muttered another curse as he headed toward the noise. He found Lady Martine pulling herself out of the water, soaking wet. Her teeth chattered, clicking together from the cold.

"Here, my lady. Take my cloak before you freeze to death." He wrapped his cloak around her and she let him do it. His hands rested on her shoulders. In the lightening sky he could see her face and the wet ends of her long hair. Her body shook. It took all his restraint not to pull her back up against him to warm her, but he wouldn't. After all, touching her is what got him into this situation in the first place.

"Thank you," she said, sounding truly grateful.

"Why did you run away?" he asked her. "It's not light yet. That was such a dangerous thing to do."

"I felt embarrassed by my actions. Why did you follow?" was her reply.

"I was trying to protect you, my lady."

They gazed into each other's eyes for a minute without either of them saying another word. For a moment, time stood still. David found himself lost in the depths of her hazel orbs. He also couldn't forget the passion she showed kissing him. It was as if she had enjoyed it. Or mayhap she just enjoyed doing things a lady should never do. He wasn't sure. After all, he'd heard stories about her and the risks she liked to take. Word traveled fast when a noble did something forbidden.

Actually, he'd heard from the wagging tongues that the entire Blake family had been acting improperly lately. It seemed that many of the Blakes were marrying from below the salt. Mayhap it was that thought that consoled him enough to try kissing her in the first place. He took one last look at her beautiful face before their time together was naught but a memory. Soon, she would return with the other nobles to the castle and forget all about him. He, on the other hand, would never forget Lady Martine.

"There, over by the creek. I see someone," came the sound of one of the guards who had been part of Lady Martine's entourage.

"Martine!" yelled out another man. There was no mistaking the deep voice of Lord Gar. The men ran toward them with their swords drawn. "Release her," commanded Gar. "Do it immediately or I will be forced to stop you by striking you down."

"What? Nay!" David jumped to the side and held up his hands. "It's not what you think. I didn't hurt her, I swear."

"Martine, there you are." Lady Josefina followed the men with Lady Regina and David's cousin, Dirk at her side. "I told my husband immediately when Regina woke me to say you were missing."

"The blind man at the door said he heard two people

leave the tavern," announced Gar. "Why did you take her, innkeeper? Why?" he shouted.

"Cousin, calm down and please, put away the weapons." Martine stepped in front of David. "This has all been a misunderstanding."

"Sister, you're soaking wet," cried Regina, rushing over and putting her arm around Martine. Josefina did the same.

"Did that man do something to you?" asked Regina.

"If so, you'd better tell Gar," said Josefina. "My husband will be sure to have him imprisoned."

"Nay, you are all wrong," Martine protested. "David didn't hurt me. Like I said, it is just a misunderstanding." Martine surprised David that she didn't tell them about the passionate kiss they'd shared or how he'd used his tongue when he realized now that he should have kept it in his mouth.

"If that's true then what are you doing out here at daybreak without an escort?" growled Gar. "You're all wet."

"I was... sleepwalking and left the tavern and fell in the creek, that's all," Martine seemed to try to convince them. "Thank goodness, David saw me leave and decided to follow. If not, I might have drowned in the river or mayhap froze to death before anyone found me."

"You call him David?" asked Gar. "Why are you speaking about him in such a familiar manner?"

"Because, that is his name." Martine turned and faced David. "Thank you, Proprietor Stone," she said, probably just to please Gar. "You have done something for me that I will never forget."

David stood there with his jaw dropped, not knowing how to respond or if he should say a word at all. He didn't want to lie to the nobles. Then again, it would be wise to follow Lady Martine's lead. He felt it was best that they kept their intimate moments between them a secret.

"Of course, my lady," said David, clearing his throat and staring at the ground. "This has been a time that I will never forget as well."

He, of course, was talking about the kisses between them. Now, David just wished he knew if that was what she meant too. Then he decided he didn't want to know, because if it wasn't what she meant, he was going to be highly disappointed.

CHAPTER 4

B y the time Martine made it back to the tavern and to David's living quarters, everyone was up for the day and already dressed. She stopped in the doorway, shocked to see Sage in clean clothes and sitting on the edge of the bed, cradling her baby.

"Sage, get back in the bed. What are you doing?" She rushed over to her friend's side. Regina and Josefina followed.

"Little Martin and I are ready to go to the castle," said Sage. She never took her eyes off the baby when she spoke.

"Martin? Is that what you named the baby?" asked Martine with a smile. "I like it."

"Yes." Finally, Sage looked up. "I named my baby after you, Martine."

"You did?" Martine was dumbfounded. The kind gesture touched her heart. "No one has ever named a baby after me. Why did you do that?"

"You were a big part in why both the baby and Lady Sage

are alive and here today," came Greta's voice from the door. She walked in with a canvas bag in her hands.

"That's right," said Sage. "I could never show you how grateful I am that you helped me. This is the least I could do."

"I am flattered." Martine's hand went to her heart. "Thank you," she said in a mere whisper as tears filled her eyes.

"Why are you wet?" Sage looked her up and down.

"It doesn't matter," answered Martine, reaching out to stroke little Martin's downy hair.

"Mother, the servant boy brought the wagon around front and is waiting." Matilda arrived at the door to the room with her sister, Cecelia.

"Well, I guess it is time for us to leave," said Josefina. "The men will be waiting for us outside."

"Leave? We're leaving? Now? So soon?" This thought made Martine feel frantic. She had hoped they'd be here another day or two. She really needed to talk to David because she didn't want him to think the kisses they shared meant nothing between them and that was why she ran from him. The real reason was because she was scared. Not of him, but by the way she'd been acting around him. While she'd enjoyed every minute of it, she realized if they were discovered, it would mean trouble for both of them. Especially for David. And when Gar got so angry when he found them by the river, she realized she had to say whatever it took to protect David. He was a kind man. A good man. A man whom she was very attracted to and whom she would like to get to know better. But now that they were leaving, she wasn't even sure if she would ever see him again.

"Yes, we're leaving for the castle," said Regina. "Sister, why do you sound as if you want to stay?"

"Yes, why do you?" asked Josefina, sounding very suspicious.

"I just thought for Sage's sake, she shouldn't be moved. Not yet." Martine felt her cheeks becoming hot. "It might be dangerous. Besides, the wagon wheel is broken."

"Nay, it's fixed," Greta told her. "Didn't anyone tell you?"

"Tell me what?" asked Martine.

"Our brother and cousin went out in the storm last night after most of us were sleeping," said Matilda.

"David and Dirk went out in the storm to fix the wagon?" she asked in shock, having had no idea.

"Yes. They fixed the wheel and brought it to the stable late last night so it wouldn't be stolen by bandits," added Cecelia.

"Really. How thoughtful of them." It surprised Martine even more that David hadn't even mentioned it to her.

"Those poor boys worked hard," added Greta. "I'll be surprised if they even had an hour of sleep. I'm going to the kitchen to make them something to eat."

Well, now Martine felt terrible, realizing why David was probably sleeping atop the table. She figured he most likely collapsed there from exhaustion after he'd returned last night to the inn. He deserved a soft bed, not the hard wood that greeted him after an even harder night.

"I still say we need to think about Sage. She shouldn't be riding in a wagon on a bumpy road so soon after giving birth." Martine tried again, but to no avail.

"I'm fine, Martine. So is little Martin." Sage smiled and cooed, talking to the baby. The baby gurgled happily in return. "Besides, I want to get to Blake Castle right away to help heal Lady Devon."

"Yes. Of course," said Martine. "We wouldn't want anything to happen to Aunt Devon."

"Get changed into something dry," her sister told her. "You can't arrive at the castle looking like that!"

"Nay, of course not. It won't take me long."

Someone cleared their throat from the door. Martine looked up to see David standing there.

"I was sent by Lord Gar to tell the ladies it is time to leave now," he told them.

"David, take this bag of food and wine to the wagon." Greta came back from the kitchen and pushed the bag into his hands. "As soon as the nobles leave, I'll make you and Dirk a big meal to break the fast. I'm sure you're hungry."

"Hungrier than you think," answered David, watching Martine with hooded eyes.

"Greta, thank you but the food is not necessary," said Martine. "The castle isn't far from here at all."

"I insist, my lady," said Greta.

"Yes, I agree," David interjected. "After all, we know how thirsty you get. I'll make sure to send some spiced wine."

A strange silence fell over the room and everyone looked at her oddly. Martine felt her body overheating.

"Well, thank you," she said to break the awkward moment. "Now if you please, I need to change for the journey."

"Of course." David bowed and left the room with his mother and sisters following.

"Martine, what was that all about?" asked Sage from the bed.

"What was what?" Martine opened her trunk and pulled out a dry gown.

"Is there something you want to tell us regarding David?" Josefina sat down on the bed next to Sage.

"I don't know what you mean. Where is that handmaid to help me change?" Martine looked around the room. They'd only brought one handmaid to share between all of them. Usually, they didn't even use handmaids because they preferred to do things themselves. However, right now she needed one as a distraction so she wouldn't have to answer Sage and Josefina's questions.

"I didn't think we needed the handmaid since we were all dressed and ready to leave," Sage told her. "I told Lavinia to meet us at the wagon."

"Regina, take little Martin to the wagon and wait for us there, will you please?" asked Sage, handing the baby to Martine's younger sister.

"Oh, I'd love to take him to the wagon. He is so sweet." Regina left the room with the baby cradled in her arms and a smile spread from ear to ear.

"Josefina, close the door," said Sage.

After she had, the room became silent. Martine laced up the bodice of her gown and looked up to see both the women staring at her.

"Why are you two looking at me as if I had two heads?" she asked.

"You like David, don't you?" asked Sage.

"Me?" She looked down and fumbled with the ties. "Well, yes, he was nice to give us his chamber. We all like him."

"Something happened between them. I know it," said

Josefina, sitting down next to Sage with a smile on her face. "I can tell by the way she is acting."

"Tell us, Martine," said Sage. "Tell us and stop making us drag it out of you."

"Nothing happened. You two are imagining things." Martine sat down to don her shoes.

"I'm sure everyone noticed your face turning red when David came to the door," said Sage.

"Yes," agreed Josefina. "And what was that little comment he made about you being so thirsty?"

Martine realized these two were going to keep pestering her about it until they got their answer. She decided to just come out and tell them.

"He kissed me," she blurted out and then slowly looked up at the other women. They both had their mouths hanging open.

"He did what?" gasped Josefina. "That is very bold for a commoner to try kissing a lady."

"Especially since he just met you," added Sage. "Martine, we've both been commoners, but know that action was highly improper."

"Not necessarily," she said with a sigh. "You see, I might have instigated the whole thing."

"What do you mean?" asked Sage.

"I kissed him first," she added and quickly stood. "Well, shall we go? Gar isn't a patient man and will be in here dragging us out by our hair if we don't hurry." She turned and started for the door.

"Stop!" commanded Josefina.

"You can't just drop that on us and then tell us nothing

more." Sage struggled to stand. Martine rushed over and she and Josefina helped her off the bed.

"Please, tell us," said Josefina.

"Don't make us beg," said Sage.

"Why did you kiss David?" asked Josefina.

"Why did you do it first?" added Sage as the three of them headed slowly to the door.

"I guess I did it because I really like him and I am tired of always being the one in the family who hasn't had a serious relationship in her life."

"Don't you mean, the one who isn't married yet?" asked Sage with a raised brow.

"Mayhap. I don't know." Martine sighed. "All I know is that I want what both of you have."

"A baby?" asked Sage.

"I don't have one of those," said Josefina.

"I'm talking about love. True love," explained Martine.

The girls stopped in their tracks.

"Martine, are you saying you are in love with David the innkeeper?" asked Josefina.

"Nay, of course not," Martine answered, feeling frustrated. "All I'm saying is that I found a man I am attracted to and would like to get to know him better. That is, before I'm handed off to some old baron to marry for alliances only."

"We understand," said Sage. "But you are a noblewoman and we were commoners."

"Yes," said Josefina. "Wouldn't marrying a commoner be moving in the wrong direction?"

"Must I remind you that my cousins, Raven, Rook, Lark, and Eleanor all married from below the salt? Besides, I never said I wanted to marry David. I just want to be able to choose the man I'll marry. I want it to be someone I feel comfortable around. Someone who makes me tingle when he kisses me. Someone who makes me feel protected when I'm in his arms." Martine looked up to the ceiling, smiling. "And someone who lights up my heart with his smile and makes me feel special."

"Like David," both Sage and Josefina said at the same time, giggling.

"What does it even matter?" asked Martine, feeling a sinking sensation in her heart. "Nothing will ever come of it, since I'll most likely never see him again once we return to the castle." This thought made her so sad. "Please, forget I even told you. Whatever you do, don't mention it to Gar or Robin or anyone else."

"All right, we won't, but you're going to marry the innkeeper, mark my words." This came from Josefina.

"Stop it. Both of you," said Martine pulling open the door. "After all, like I said, I'll never even see David again."

"You could if you wanted to," insisted Sage.

"I am a lady," she told them, becoming solemn. "There is no reason in hell for me to even be in a tavern if I'm not traveling with male escorts. So even if I did return to the Cross Hare Inn, David and I would never be alone."

"We both found ways to be alone with our husbands before we were married," said Josefina, nodding to Sage.

"Yes. I healed Robin."

"I hired Gar to sail my trade ship," Josefina reminded her.

"You both had jobs that brought you together with your husbands. That'll never happen for me. I don't have a job.

My job is just being a lady and marrying a noble and bearing him male heirs."

"Don't give up on him," said Sage. "If you two really want to be together, I'm certain you will find a way."

"I wish that were true, but I'm not so sure about that," answered Martine, knowing there was nothing she could possibly do to bring her back here to David Stone.

David watched the nobles disappear down the road and raised his hand to wave goodbye. He and his family were there to see them off.

"Well, now that they're gone, we can get back to normal," said Joe, clinging to Greta's arm as they turned to go back to the inn.

"I, for one, felt very uncomfortable with them staying in our quarters," Dirk told the others. "I didn't like it."

"I didn't mind. I felt comfortable around them," said Matilda. "Even if they were nobles."

"I liked them, too." Cecelia rubbed her broadening belly as they walked. "I am glad we helped them. If that was me birthing my baby in that situation, I'd welcome any help I could get. Commoners, or not."

"Step it up," his mother called back over her shoulder. "David, you'll need to haul your pallet outside and burn it since it is soiled with blood."

"Aye," he answered, not really caring about pallets at the moment. He didn't think he'd feel so sad when Martine left, but he truly did. Since they'd kissed and talked, he felt like all nobles weren't alike. Martine was special. She didn't look down on commoners the way the rest of the nobles did. She was easy to talk to and made him feel comfortable around her. Yes, Martine was a special lady and he wasn't going to easily forget her.

"Dirk, help David with the pallet. I'll keep an eye on the tavern if anyone should come in," his Uncle Joe offered.

"Yes, you keep an eye on things," said David with a chuckle. Even though the man was blind, there wasn't anything that got past him.

They entered the tavern and made their way to the living quarters.

"Those girls weren't hard to look at," said Dirk with a chuckle as they entered the room.

"Those girls are ladies," David corrected him. "Show some respect. And quit talking about them because they were married." David bent down and picked up the pallet, throwing it over his shoulder, not needing Dirk's help.

"Not that Lady Martine. She was fine and not married. I wouldn't have blamed you if you really did take her out by the creek to have your way with her. I'll bet she is a real vixen in bed."

"Shut up! She's not like that." David threw the pallet at Dirk, catching him by surprise and knocking him to the floor.

"What's got you so uptight?" grumbled Dirk. "We always talk about the girls that come into the tavern."

"Martine is not just a girl. She's a lady, and I'll not hear you say another word about her or I'll bust you in the mouth. Understand?"

"Ooooooh, I see." Dirk got up and brushed off his tunic. "I got a little too close to home, did I? Sorry. I didn't know you fancied the girl or I wouldn't have said anything about her." He threw the pallet over his shoulder and headed to the door.

"I don't fancy anyone. I just think you need to be more respectful of the nobles, that's all."

"Is that really it?" Dirk looked over his shoulder as he headed out the door. "Keep telling yourself that, Cousin, and mayhap you'll someday believe it. However, you're never going to convince me that you don't have the same thoughts swarming around in your head about the girl that I have."

"I said, stop calling her a girl."

"Holy hell, you've got it bad," said Dirk, repositioning the pallet on his shoulder. "It's just too damned bad you'll never see the girl, I mean, the lady again."

As Dirk left with the pallet, David realized that his cousin was right. The kisses they'd shared had been stupid on his part. Just thinking about it was always going to get him hot and bothered. After kissing Lady Martine, not even Cinnamon the whore would be able to suffice the burning he felt inside for the noblewoman. She was a woman he could never have because they were from two different worlds and would always be.

CHAPTER 5

"I feel so much better. Thank you, everyone for coming to my aid." Lady Devon, wife of Lord Corbett Blake sat up in her bed the next morning with an entourage of ladies surrounding her.

"I knew if I could get here, I'd have the proper herbs to heal you." Sage sat on the bed next to Lady Devon, handing her a goblet from which to drink more of her healing potion.

Devon took a sip and handed the goblet back to Sage. "I am only happy that you are all right, Sage. As well as baby Martin. Won't Robin and the men be surprised when they return from battle to find out Robin has an heir?"

"Yes, they will be." Sage handed her the goblet to drink again. "Here, have more of my healing potion so your strength will return quickly."

"Thank you." Devon took a sip of the potion, glancing over the edge of the cup. "Martine, you are so quiet. Is everything all right, dear?"

"Huh?" Martine was deep in her thoughts and hadn't

even paid any attention to the conversation going on around her. She kept trying to figure out a way to see David again, but couldn't. "Yes. Yes, I'm fine, thank you."

"The innkeeper and his family were kind enough to give us shelter from the storm," said Josefina, pulling open the shutters for some air. "If it weren't for them, Sage's baby might have been born in a puddle."

"Or not at all," Sage added. "We need to show our gratitude to them, as well as to you, Martine. Greta couldn't have done it without you."

"Me?" Martine looked over to the others. "Nay, I only did what any good sister-by-marriage would do. It is Greta and her family who deserve the true thanks."

"Yes, they should be rewarded," agreed Devon.

"They gave up their living quarters for us," explained Sage. "Oh, I almost forgot. I would like to have a new pallet sent to the inn since I ruined David's bed giving birth to little Martin."

"David?" asked Devon.

"David Stone. He's the proprietor of the Cross Hare Inn. Right, Martine?" Sage smiled, looking over at Martine.

"Yes. That's correct," she answered, roaming over to the window and glancing out, still feeling sad.

"Well, they need to be rewarded. I'll make sure to have one of my guards deliver not only a new pallet but a frame to make a nice bed," offered Devon.

"I think we need to do a little more than that." It was Sage pushing but Martine didn't stop her.

"If you mean, send them money, I'm afraid Corbett would never approve of that," said Devon. "I'd have to check the ledgers of course, but I believe the Cross Hare Inn is one of the establishments that owes us many months of rent."

"I didn't mean money," said Sage.

"What would you suggest then?" asked Devon.

"I know," said Josefina, hurrying over to the bed. "Why don't we invite David and his family here to the castle to join us for a meal?"

"I suppose there would be no harm in that," agreed Devon.

"What? Nay," said Martine, turning around and hurrying over to the bed. "I don't think that is a good idea at all."

"Well, I think it is a splendid one." Devon handed Sage the goblet. "I'll send a messenger at once to invite them to join us tomorrow at midday for a meal."

"Nay, Lord Corbett wouldn't approve." Martine felt panicked by this thought. Seeing David at the inn was one thing but bringing him into her world might make him feel inferior and she didn't want that. Nay, she couldn't have David or his family at the castle. He'd be treated as a lowly commoner and made to eat below the salt with the servants. In the meantime, she would be dressed in the finest of clothes and sitting at the dais looking down on him and his family. Martine felt something for this man. It would break her heart to see him treated in this manner even if it was proper of commoners to eat below the salt.

"Corbett isn't here to object, and it is only a harmless meal. We invite villagers and peasants into the castle all the time to eat. I say we do it and that is final," announced Devon. "I'll make certain to send a messenger to the Cross Hare Inn at once with a missive to invite them."

"They have an inn to run. They are very busy. They won't be able to join us," said Martine, shaking her head.

"We can send some of our servants over to help out at the inn until they return from the feast if need be," suggested Sage, trying to be ever so helpful. Actually, Martine realized that she and Josefina were trying to bring Martine and David back together, but Martine didn't want it to happen this way.

"It'll only be midday and their busiest time is at night, so it should be fine," added Josefina, looking just as happy with her plan as Sage was right now.

Martine groaned inwardly. There was no way she was going to stop three women who had their minds already made up. It was obvious she wasn't going to be able to change things in the least. Mayhap she should be glad since this was definitely a way to see David again. Still, she didn't feel as if she wanted him here. It would only point out the big difference in their statuses. She would much rather have seen him again in his surroundings where he felt truly comfortable. Bringing him here was only going to make him realize how different from each other they really were.

There was a quick knock on the door and Lady Devon's twins, Raven and Rook, entered the room dressed in long cloaks as if they'd just arrived at the castle.

"Mother, how are you feeling?" asked Rook, hurrying to her side.

"I am fine, Rook. Thanks to Sage and her healing herbs, that is."

"Hello, Martine," said Raven. "I haven't seen you in a while." Raven had long black hair. Her brother had black hair as well. Raven married a blacksmith and Rook married his lady gardener.

"Hello," Martine answered with a nod. "Have you two seen Sage's new baby yet?"

"Yes," said Rook. "Rose is in the great hall right now holding the baby so tightly I'm afraid no one will be able to pry him away from her. She may never give the poor boy back to the nursemaid."

"I didn't know your wife liked babies so much," said Martine in surprise.

"She does now," mumbled Raven.

"Well, you should too," Rook told his sister. "After all you are in the same condition as her."

"What condition is that?" asked Sage.

"Rose and Raven are both pregnant. Didn't you know?" said Devon. "I'm going to have grandchildren and I couldn't be happier."

"What?" asked Josefina, Sage, and Martine at the same time.

"Raven, are you really going to have a baby?" asked Martine.

"Yes, it seems so," said Raven with a nod. Any other woman would have seemed overjoyed. Raven, on the other hand, looked somewhat pleased but not ecstatic. Then again, the girl had been raised as a warrior, like her twin brother. It was her choice to wield a sword and she could do it as well as any man. Nothing much scared Raven. However, Martine figured being a mother was foreign to her and this was out of her element. Raven was going to have to learn all the skills of a lady now, and that could prove quite terrifying. After all, the girl had fought it most of her life.

"Jonathon and I just found out we're having a baby and we couldn't be happier." She actually smiled this time.

"Since we're twins, you know we tend to do things at the same time," said Rook. "Rose is due around the same time as Raven."

"My, this family is growing quickly. I can't wait for my grandchildren to be born." Devon swung her feet over the side of the bed.

"Mother, where do you think you're going?" asked Rook. "You need to rest."

"I can't. With Corbett away, I have duties to tend to since I am Lady of the Castle."

"I'll handle them," Rook assured her. "Now, I want to see you get back in bed and stay there for a while. You were very sick lately and we weren't even sure we wouldn't lose you."

"Rook, you have your own manor to tend to," Devon told him, reaching out and touching her son on the arm. "I don't want to trouble you. Especially now that you and Rose are going to have a baby. It is too much to ask."

"I told Father I'd handle things at Blake Castle until he returns," stated Rook. "Plus, I'm sure Raven will help me."

"Yes, of course, I will." Raven was not one to be dismissed easily. She could handle anything. The girl was truly amazing and even knew how to joust. She was an inspiration to Martine.

"I'll take care of the garrison and training the knights if Raven oversees the kitchen and collects the rents in town," said Rook. "Some of the commoners are far behind in their payments. Father told me he was going to have to take away some of the businesses from the proprietors if they couldn't get caught up with what they owed us."

That took Martine's interest. She'd heard her aunt say that the Cross Hare Inn was way behind in paying their rent. She didn't want David to lose his business.

"I want to help out too while Uncle Corbett and Robin are away," said Martine. "I will assist Raven in collecting the rents in town. I can also handle inventory in the undercroft and balancing the ledgers. I do it all the time at home."

"That is thoughtful of you, Martine," said Devon. "You will make a good wife and lady of the castle someday with all your skills. But aren't you planning on going back home to be with your mother until your father returns from battle?"

"Nay. Not yet."

"Why not?" asked Rook. "I'm sure your mother could use your help in your father's absence."

"My mother will have no problem handling things while he is away. My youngest sister, Dorothy is there and I'll be sure to send Regina home to help her as well."

"Why Regina and not you?" asked Rook, not letting up.

"Martine has other things that interest her right here in Steepleton for the moment." Sage smiled knowingly.

Martine cringed, hoping that neither Sage or Josefina would leak her secret. She didn't need Rook giving her grief about having eyes for an innkeeper. He should understand Martine's interest in a commoner since Rook married his gardener. Still, she didn't want to risk it. Especially since she wasn't even sure if anything would ever come of the kisses she had shared with David.

"What other things? What does that mean, Martine? Is there something I should know?" Rook fired questions at her left and right. Martine felt as if she were being interrogated.

"The only thing you should know, my dear cousin, is that I want to be helpful for Aunt Devon's sake. Plus, if Sage is here with baby Martin, I want to help out with his care as well."

"Sage, do you really want to stay here at Blake Castle until Corbett, your father, and Robin return?" asked Devon.

"Yes, I do."

"I'd like her to stay here too since I might need her," Sage answered, most likely just trying to help her see David again. "After all, Martine is good with birthing babies now."

That comment startled Martine. Her stomach turned just remembering what she'd gone through. "I can't say it's anything I'd ever want to do again, but I don't mind watching over little Martin now that he's born. I'll do so whenever you need it," answered Martine.

"With all the good news about the baby and babies-to-be, why don't we invite the rest of your cousins here to celebrate?" Josefina asked Martine, Rook, and Raven. "After all, they will all be excited to see Sage and Robin's baby."

"Yes, I agree. We haven't all been together for a while now," added Sage.

"That is a wonderful idea," said Devon. "We'll have a large feast and invite everyone we know. It'll take place as soon as the men return."

"Be sure to invite Lark," said Raven. "She can bring Dustin and Florie." Raven spoke of the Scottish girl's husband and daughter. "Besides, she's pregnant again too. We'll have a lot to talk about. I have things to ask her." Raven's hand went to her stomach and she looked as if she felt ill.

"This is going to be wonderful." Devon scooched back

onto the bed, smiling from ear to ear. "We'll have a real family reunion."

"Then you'll stay in bed for at least a few more days, Mother?" Rook asked in concern.

"I, as your healer, suggest you do so until you are stronger, Lady Devon," said Sage. "I will be staying right here at your beside until the men return."

"Since all of you are so willing to help out, I don't see how I can say no." Devon looked over at Martine. "Martine, you know the Stone family now so will you please go with the messenger when he drops off the pallet and missive asking them to join us for a meal? I think at least one of us should show up with the invitation."

Martine fought against everything that warned her not to do it. Still, she had just told Lady Devon she'd help out in any way she could, so how could she refuse? If only she had given her a different chore right now, it might be better. Martine wasn't sure she was ready to see David again, even if it was really what she wanted. She felt her stomach flutter.

"Of course, my lady," she said forcing a smile and giving her aunt a small nod. "Whatever you wish."

Martine looked over to see Sage and Josefina grinning devilishly. They'd succeeded with their plan. Now, if only Martine could be happy about this as well. This really wasn't what she had in mind when she decided she wanted to meet back up with the handsome and very kissable David Stone. She hoped it would be on more common ground, not inviting him to the castle where he would feel even more common than ever.

CHAPTER 6

"David, I hear horses approaching. By the jangle of the tack I'd say it is nobles." Uncle Joe stood at the open door of the inn, his ear cocked, listening to the sound.

"Tell them we're not open yet," growled David, flipping the last of the coins he'd been counting into the cash chest. He closed the lid and then slammed shut his leather-bound ledger, shoving them into the secret compartment and using the key to lock it.

"David, what's got you in such a bad mood this morning?" Dirk walked into the tavern from their living quarters, stretching and yawning.

"Besides the fact I had to sleep on the hard wooden table again last night, you mean?" David picked up his apron, tying it around himself. It covered his chest as well as the front of his clothes. He rung out a rag in a bucket of water and pushed past his cousin, starting to wipe down the tables.

"Just buy a pallet if that's what's bothering you," said Dirk.

"With what?" David scrubbed the stains of last night's spilled porridge and ale from a table. "We don't have enough money for such things."

"Even after the crowd we had in here the night of the storm?" Joe asked from the doorway.

"Even so."

"I thought we'd bring in good coin that night," said Dirk.

"We did." David walked over and started to clean another table. "But after paying for all the damages from a crowd that size, and after having to feed all the nobles, we are even more behind than before."

"Are you sure?" asked Dirk, squinting and scratching the stubble on his jaw. "I didn't notice that when I did the ledgers."

"You can't read and can barely add," David told him. "I never should have let you attempt balancing the ledgers because you messed things up and now I am scrambling to fix them."

"Stop your quarreling boys." Joe closed the door and used his walking stick to tap the ground, making his way over to them. "The nobles are about to enter. Hopefully, we can make some good coin off of them."

"We don't open until this afternoon," said David, loading dirty cups onto a tray. "Where the hell are my sisters? This place needs a good cleaning before we can open for business."

"Your sisters and mother left early this morning," said Joe. "They went to the alehouse to help the alewives since we are extremely low on wine and ale. When they help, the price charged to us is less."

"They did? Why didn't anyone tell me?" David didn't like anything going on in his inn that he didn't know about.

"You were sleeping soundly on the table and they didn't want to wake you," said Joe. David didn't need to look up to know that both Joe and Dirk were smiling about that.

The door to the tavern banged open and a messenger wearing the banner of Blake Castle entered the room.

"The tavern is not open this early, I'm sorry," David said, picking up the overloaded tray of empty drinking vessels and dirty wooden bowls. "You'll have to leave and come back later," he said, not bothering to look up.

"We're not here as customers," came a very familiar female voice that he hadn't been able to stop thinking about. He looked up to see Lady Martine walking over to him. "Good morning, David."

Her long velvet gown and fur-lined cloak swept over the floor as she glided toward him looking like a radiant queen. Suddenly, his nerves got the best of him. He felt disheveled and dirty. He hadn't even combed his hair this morning. Why was she here and what did she want? He thought he'd never see her again.

"Lady Martine. How can I help you?" With his attention on the girl instead of his tray, the cups and bowls shifted. He hurried to right them, ending up with most of them clattering to the floor. "Damn," he spat, hurriedly sliding the tray onto the table and bending down to collect the spilled dishes.

"Surprised to see me?" The noblewoman hunkered down and started to pick up the cups from the floor along with him. This was surely not the way a noble should act. What was the matter with her?

David closed his eyes, not able to believe what she was doing. "Get up," he said in a half-whisper, not wanting the others to see her helping a mere commoner. He wasn't even a noble, and her action embarrassed him.

"What?" she asked, as if she didn't understand.

"My lady, it isn't proper for you to do that." The guard was at her side immediately, helping her to her feet.

"Why are you here?" David asked once again, taking the dirty cups from Martine and quickly standing. "Did you mayhap forget something in my living quarters?"

"Nay," she answered. "We come bearing gifts."

"Gifts?" He wasn't sure what she meant, but thought this had something to do with the kisses they'd shared. Damn it, was she rewarding him for doing something that had been stupid on his part, not to mention highly forbidden? "Nay, it's not necessary. Please, don't even think—" He stopped in midsentence when the door opened wider and a servant strolled in carrying a pallet over his shoulder.

"Oh, that," he said, clearing his throat. "Yes. Gifts."

"You seem surprised," she said. "What did you think I meant?"

"I wasn't sure."

"Lady Sage felt bad about ruining your bed," Martine continued. "Please accept not only a new pallet but a new bed in total." Martine waved her arm through the air and another two servants entered carrying what looked like a wooden bedframe, more elegant than anything he'd ever owned. "Go right through the kitchen," she instructed the servants. "There is a room attached with the living quarters."

"Aye, my lady," answered one of the servants.

"Thank you," said David, feeling so choked up at the moment that he could barely speak. Just being in her presence made him feel excited yet uneasy all at the same time.

"You are the proprietor, David Stone?" asked the guard, taking a folded parchment from his pouch at his waist.

"I am," said David.

"Lady Devon of Blake Castle asked me to deliver this missive to you." The guard handed it to David and he took it.

"What is this?" asked David.

"It's an invitation," said Martine before the guard could even answer.

"Invitation? To what?" David stared at the folded missive stamped with a wax seal, feeling dumbfounded. Not he, nor any of his family had ever had an invitation from the castle before.

"You may leave now, Dexter." Martine dismissed the guard who left through the front door. Then she directed her focus to David. "It's our way of thanking you and your family."

"Thanking us?" he asked, still staring at the closed missive, for some reason feeling apprehensive to open it.

"Yes. For giving us shelter and lending us your living quarters when we were in great need," explained Martine.

"Of course. I see." He took a deep breath and released it, wondering about this whole situation.

"God's eyes, David. What are you waiting for? Open it," said the blind man, hobbling over. "If I could see, I'd read it myself."

"I can't wait to see what it says." Dirk hurried over and ripped the missive out of David's hand. David didn't even flinch. He still felt numb for some reason.

"Wouldn't you like to read it yourself?" Martine asked him, sounding disappointed that he wasn't doing so.

"He'll give it back to me," said David, not sounding at all concerned. "Dirk doesn't know how to read."

"Dammit, take it." Dirk pushed the missive back into David's hand and took his father's arm. "Let's go to the kitchen and get something to eat," he told Joe.

When Dirk and Joe exited the room, it left Martine alone with him now. David slowly opened the missive, his eyes quickly scanning the contents.

Martine's stomach flip-flopped as she watched David reading the missive with no expression at all on his face. She had hoped he'd feel elated to be invited to the castle. Any commoner getting an invitation from a noble would be. David was different. Suddenly, she started thinking this wasn't a good idea for her to come here after all. It wasn't actually her choice, but she hadn't resisted since she really wanted to see David again.

"Lady Devon is inviting you and your family to a meal at the castle tomorrow at midday," she told him, even though he'd just read the missive for himself. She was searching for a reaction of any kind from him but had yet to get it.

"I know, my lady. I can read." He very carefully folded the missive back up and stuck it into his waistband, heading back to the table and continuing to pick up the tray of dirty dishes as if none of this had happened.

"I wasn't insinuating that you can't read," she said, following him across the room. "I just was waiting for you to respond to the very generous and kind offer."

Without saying a word, he stepped around her and started for the kitchen.

"Well?" asked Martine. "Will you and your family be there? I'll have to give Lady Devon a reply."

"You can tell Lady Devon that my family will be happy to join her."

"Your family?" she asked in confusion. "You mean you too then. Right?"

He stopped and talked to her without turning to look. "I'm not sure," he answered.

"Not sure?" she asked, feeling alarmed. "You don't want to come to the castle?"

"It's not that. I just... can't." He started to leave, but Martine took his arm from behind.

"I know this won't be easy, David, but it is a chance for us to see each other again."

"I didn't think I'd ever see you again," he said softly.

"Neither did I. And although this isn't the way I'd like it to happen, at least we won't be apart."

"I see."

"So, will you join your family then? Will you come to eat at the castle?"

As he considered it, she couldn't stop thinking that it would only put a bigger wedge between them.

"Nay, my lady, I am afraid I will have to decline the offer."

Her hand slowly slipped from his arm, her heart hurting worse than it already did.

"It's because of me, isn't it?"

"I have an inn to run. I cannot be taking precious time off when there is so much work to be done."

Martine didn't understand David's answer and wasn't sure what to say to him. Was his time so precious that he chose his inn over being with her? That made her feel angry. She told him it wasn't the ideal way to be together, but at least they'd get to see one another. Still, he didn't seem interested. She supposed she couldn't blame him. Now she regretted having come to deliver the missive and wished Sage and Josefina had never suggested this at all.

"We can send servants from the castle to do the work while you and your family join us for the feast." She decided to make it impossible for him to say no now. Martine wanted to give him every opportunity to continue the relationship with her that he had started.

David slowly turned his head and looked over his shoulder as he answered. "And what will Lord Corbett say when he finds out that you are entertaining a family who is behind in paying their rent? I hardly think he will agree to this type of generosity."

"Oh, is that what's bothering you?" she asked, wondering if she'd read him wrong. "Don't worry about that, David. My uncle is not here right now. Besides, it was my aunt's idea to invite you. So why does it even matter?"

"It matters to me," he said softly.

"But this is Lady Devon's way of showing gratitude for what you did for Lady Sage. For all of us."

"I appreciate the offer, but we need money, not food."

"This has nothing to do with your overdue rent. It has everything to do with Lady Sage and her baby."

"I understand."

"So, you'll come with your family to eat at the castle then?"

"Out of respect for Lady Devon, I will send the rest of my family to dine with you. They deserve a good meal at the castle," said David. "However, I still have to decline the offer. I cannot leave my inn. I'm sorry."

"I see," she said, her gaze slowly falling to her feet. Mayhap she should be happy he wouldn't be joining them since it would only make her feel awkward to have him there after all. But when he refused the offer, she couldn't help feeling as if he were refusing her personally and that didn't feel good at all. "I'm sorry you feel that way, David. I really am."

"Please give my regards to Lady Devon and also relay my thanks for the new bed."

She wasn't going to let him off that easy. Not when his decision affected her as well. "I will not. I am a noble, not your personal messenger. If you'd like to give my aunt a message, then do so yourself." Martine almost felt as if she were about to cry, but fought hard to maintain her composure. She turned to leave, but David's voice stopped her.

"Martine," he said, making her heart jump as she stopped in her tracks and slowly turned around. "I mean, Lady Martine," he said, still balancing the tray on his hand. His eyes looked so sad, his face so sullen. "I'm truly sorry."

"So am I," she answered, feeling her heart breaking. After what they'd shared together, Martine had hoped to get to know David better. She had hoped he'd have feelings for her the same as she did for him. It seems she was mistaken about him after all. "Ladies Josefina and Sage will be disappointed as well that you aren't there." She quickly added the latter because she didn't want to let him know how much his refusal upset her.

"That's not what I mean." His eyes closed briefly and then reopened. He seemed perplexed. As if he was struggling for his words. Then he looked up to the ceiling and she saw a vein throbbing at his neck. "What I mean is that you don't have to do this."

"Don't have to do what? I don't understand." She took a few steps toward him.

"It was a mistake, my lady. What happened between us never should have transpired and we both know it. I am truly sorry that things couldn't be different, but we both know they can't."

The knife in her heart from his refusal now twisted sharply. "You are talking about the kisses," she said boldly, not really caring if anyone heard.

"Shhh," he warned her, quickly glancing over his shoulder. "I don't want anyone to hear."

"Nay. I suppose you don't," she said, ready to shout it aloud just to make him feel as uncomfortable as she did at the moment.

"I never should have done it. It was wrong of me. I'm not sure why I did."

She didn't like this sudden false act of modesty. David didn't seem like the kind of man who would ever apologize for his actions. "You act as if our actions were your decision only, when they were warranted by both of us," she pointed out.

"Please," he said, his eyes closing and opening once again. "Only I am to blame. You don't need to say that."

"I don't say things only to make one feel better," she told him. "I say exactly what I mean."

"Lady Martine, I can't— I mean we can't see each other again. It's not proper. If word leaks out about what happened, I could be punished. Mayhap even imprisoned."

"Is that what you're worried about?" she asked, disgusted that he was only thinking about himself. "Funny, but I didn't take you for a coward, David."

"Coward?" His brows dipped and he walked toward her, leaving the tray of dishes on the drink board. "I assure you, my lady, I am quite braver than you might believe."

"I don't see that, I'm afraid. I see a man who is so scared of the potential consequences that he's afraid to even admit his own feelings."

He jerked back, her words seeming to surprise him. Then he shook his head and spoke with no emotion at all in his voice. "I'm sorry you think that way about me but I am only doing what I need to do in order to protect my family. I can't take the risk of something happening to me. If something did happen to me, that would leave them in a very bad position." He continued to walk toward her as he spoke. "Since my father's death, all responsibility has fallen upon my shoulders. It is a heavy burden to bear, although I can't expect you to understand."

"I resent that remark. I am not as insensitive to people's feelings as you make it sound."

"This inn is my family's life, my lady. It is the blood that flows through our veins. Without it, we are nothing. I cannot and will not lose it because of my own careless actions. I will take every precaution, use every spare minute I have, to do whatever I can to provide for my family."

"Your desire to help your family is admirable, but I resent you referring to what happened between us as naught but careless actions. Be careful not to lose yourself along the way," she told him.

"What does that mean?" He stopped now, standing before her.

"Your words speak of your inn and your family only. Is there nothing else you care about besides that?" She wanted him to say he had felt something for her when they'd kissed. Martine wanted more than anything for David to tell her he wanted to see her again, even if they had to do so in secret. But instead, he was dismissing her from his life as if she and their shared intimate moments never even happened.

"I'm sorry, but that is all it can ever be," he told her, his eyes staring at her lips. Her senses were reeling, telling her he really wanted to kiss her again but wouldn't risk it. "You are a lady and I am naught but a commoner."

"I know that."

"We don't belong together, my lady. I was wrong when I– when we did what we did. We need to put it behind us now because it will only bring both of us pain and discomfort."

"I didn't feel pain or discomfort when we kissed. Didn't it mean anything at all to you?"

He was quiet for a moment. His gaze traveled up from her lips to her eyes and stopped there. She saw his turmoil within. Part of her wanted to comfort him, but at this point she didn't know how.

"Nay," he said so quietly that she almost thought she'd imagined it. "It meant nothing. Nothing at all, my lady."

The knife in her heart sank in deeper, going for the kill.

Now, her anger was stronger than her hurt and she wanted more than anything to give him a piece of her mind. It took every bit of her strength to refrain from telling him he was the biggest liar she'd ever met. Martine knew he had felt something between them when they'd kissed, just as she had. But before she could confront him, a door slammed open from a room upstairs and the tavern whore came bounding down the stairs.

"David?" The whore stopped when she saw Martine. "What's going on?" She glared at Martine as if she was disgusted that she was there, or mayhap as if she were jealous.

"Cinnamon, please take this to the kitchen." He hurried over and picked up the tray and held it out to her. The girl didn't take it. Instead, she kept staring at Martine, making Martine feel very uncomfortable.

"I'm not a scullery maid, David, and you know it." Her hand rested on his shoulder and she let her fingers slowly slide down his arm. "Now, if you need something else, you know I'm always here to give it to you."

It was too much for Martine to watch. She was sure David had bedded the whore in the past but at this moment seeing the girl touch him so intimately made her heart drop in her chest. Martine wanted to be the girl on David's arm, but he didn't want her. She couldn't even imagine that hussy kissing or making love to the man that she had lost her heart to after just one kiss.

Martine turned and ran from the tavern, not stopping until she reached her horse.

"My lady?" asked Dexter, looking up in surprise. "Is something wrong? You seem flustered."

The servants exited the tavern, returning to the horse and cart after having delivered and set up the bed.

"It's time to go," she said, not waiting for Dexter to help her mount her steed. Right now she didn't want any man to touch her.

"Lady Martine, wait!" called out David from the door to the tavern. The whore stood right behind him, looking over his shoulder. Martine didn't want him to see the tears welling in her eyes and so she ignored him. Just like he wanted to pretend their kisses never happened, she refused to answer him and instead acted as if he was the one who didn't exist now.

"Yaw!" she called to the horse, kicking her heels into the sides of the animal, and speeding away without looking back.

It was over between her and David and she knew it now. It was over before it ever really began. He wasn't willing to risk his neck for her. If not, then she wanted nothing to do with him again. When she fell in love with a man she needed that man to be willing to walk through fire for her without even blinking. Martine wanted the kind of love she'd seen between her cousins and their spouses and between her brother Robin and the healer, Sage. That was true love. Love that she wanted more than anything in her life right now. Sadly, she realized that she might never find it. Her feelings for David would have to be pushed aside since when her father returned she was sure he would betroth her to a noble. That is, a man who was proper and a good match. A form of alliance and having nothing to do with feelings or emotions.

"Damn you, David Stone," she spat, feeling the harsh

wind sting her face as her tears flowed down her cheeks. She didn't care. Martine's inner pain was far worse than anything she would or could feel physically. "Damn you to hell," she said through gritted teeth feeling like the biggest fool to walk the earth. Just because he'd kissed her, it meant nothing at all to him. And now that she knew the truth, she was dreading having to tell Sage and Josefina that she'd never find the kind of love they'd found, because it was over for her. David Stone was naught but a meaningless flirtation in the night and they would never, could never, end up together.

CHAPTER 7

"**M**artine, where is David? I don't see him," said Sage the next day, stretching her neck as the nobles sat at the dais waiting for the meal to be served.

Josefina leaned over to talk to the two of them. "I see David's cousin and his blind uncle. Even his mother and two sisters are sitting down there below the salt. No David."

"Mayhap he's just late," whispered Sage, sounding as if she was trying to make Martine feel better.

"I'm sure that's it. I suppose he might have had things to take care of at the tavern first," Josefina added with a nod.

"He's not coming." Martine picked up her goblet and held it out to the cup bearer. "Is that mead?" she asked.

"Nay, my lady," answered the boy. "It is white wine. Did you want me to ask in the buttery if any mead is available?"

"Never mind," she said with a nod, so upset she'd even drink white wine though she didn't care for it. "Just fill it to the top, please."

Once Martine had her wine, Lady Raven and Lord Rook stood up and motioned for silence.

"We speak for our parents, Lord Corbett and Lady Devon," said Rook in a loud voice so everyone could hear them.

"Our father is away serving the king and our mother is recovering from a serious illness. We've convinced her to stay in bed and rest instead of joining us here today. It is for precautionary measures, even though, thanks to Lady Sage she is recovering nicely," Raven told them.

"Yes, that's right." Rook raised his goblet. "However, she wanted me to introduce everyone to our guests today, the Stone family. They were the ones who helped members of my family lately."

"Yes," said Sage, standing as well. "I was having my baby and they gave us shelter at the Cross Hare Inn. Greta Stone, along with our own Lady Martine helped to deliver my baby." Clapping and cheers went up from the crowd. "Please meet the heir of Robin Blake, little Martin." She nodded and the nursemaid stood up, holding up the baby. The crowd clapped and cheered some more.

"Martine," said Raven, trying to get her attention. "Martine, we'd like you to introduce the Stone family now."

"What?" Martine was sipping her wine and almost choked on it. She had no idea she was going to be put in this position. It made her uncomfortable.

"Go on," Josefina urged her as Raven and Rook sat. "Everyone is waiting."

Martine was about to get up when a man standing in the archway of the great hall took her attention. She glanced up to see David arrive, stopping in the doorway but not entering the room. He looked over at Martine and their eyes locked. Then he quickly dropped his gaze and turned to leave.

Martine needed to do something quickly. "We'd like to thank the proprietor of the Cross Hare Inn, David Stone," Martine said loudly, standing up with her goblet raised in the air.

The crowd cheered and looked around for David.

"David?" Martine glanced over at him, seeing the surprised look on his face. "Please, come join your mother, Greta, sisters, Cecelia and Matilda, as well as your Uncle Joe and Cousin Dirk. This meal is our way of saying thank you for what all of you did for my family."

The crowd clapped and cheered and some of the men even whistled. Greta and her family looked around, smiling at the others. Her plan worked. David couldn't leave now since everyone was staring at him standing in the doorway.

"David, come join us," called out his cousin, Dirk.

Slowly, he walked into the room keeping his head down. His younger sister waved to him and his mother looked very pleased that he had joined them after all. David squeezed in between his sisters on the wooden bench at a table set up below the salt.

The meal was anything but enjoyable as far as Martine was concerned. Part of her now wished that David had stayed at the inn after all. He sat with his back to her, purposely she decided. His family ate with the servants and commoners while she was raised up with the nobles, looking down at those below the salt.

Martine had a moment when she thought about not even introducing David. After all, he seemed as if he were going to leave instead of joining his family. But wanting him to feel as uncomfortable as she'd felt after he told her their kisses meant nothing at all to him, she'd purposely called out his name. That made it impossible for him to leave. A part of her still felt sorry for him but the vengeful feelings stirring within her since he'd made her feel like a fool were somehow satisfied by this. Martine didn't know where this was coming from. She didn't like purposely being mean to others.

"Martine, I'm so glad we ended up being friends," Sage told her. "After all, when we first met, I was sure you hated me."

That brought back memories that Martine had nearly forgotten about. She was right. Martine hadn't liked Sage at all when they first met.

"Robin was wrong calling you judgmental," Sage continued. "You have been so kind to David and his family, not judging them at all for being commoners, and that proves it."

"Yes. Kind," said Martine, feeling ill at the thought of the way she used to be. At one time Martine had been horribly judgmental and extremely mean to those who weren't of her same status. Was she going back to being that person again? She wondered. It didn't feel good to think that she might be doing exactly that. Her emotions were out of control lately. She needed to be careful not to slip back to her old ways because that was not the person she wanted to be.

Every so often Martine looked down from the dais to see David peering back over his shoulder at her. Then they'd both quickly direct their attention in the opposite directions. Neither one of them smiled at all.

"For heaven's sake, go over and talk to him," Sage whispered in her ear.

"Yes," agreed Josefina from her other side. "This is your chance to spend time with the man you fancy."

"I don't know," Martine answered, feeling very sad. "I'm no longer sure I even like him," David's presence at the castle had her feeling very confused right now. Why had he even showed up here today after telling her he had work to do? He made it sound as if to accept the invitation was nothing more than a bother.

"What do you mean you might no longer like him?" asked Josefina. "When did this come about?"

"David told me something yesterday that changed everything."

"What are you talking about?" asked Sage. The two women leaned in closer to hear her since she wasn't speaking very loudly, not wanting anyone to eavesdrop.

"Explain," said Josefina directly.

"David said that what we shared meant nothing at all to him. He also said that he didn't want to see me ever again."

"Nay! That can't be true," said Sage in shock. "If so he wouldn't be here now, would he?"

Martine was curious about the real reason why David had come to the castle after all. She also wondered if mayhap he almost didn't come since he hadn't arrived here with the rest of his family. Still, she decided she wasn't going ask him. Nay, she didn't want to talk to him at all.

The minstrels started playing music, and the tables below the salt were cleared and moved, making room for people to dance.

"Now is your big chance, Martine," said Josefina. "Go and ask him to dance."

"What? Are you crazy?" Martine's heart sped up just hearing the suggestion. "I can't do that."

"Why not?" asked Sage. "Just because he is from below the salt?"

"It wouldn't be proper," Martine told them, glancing down the table at the other nobles. "I just can't."

"Do what you will or won't, but I am going to dance with my husband." Josefina got up and walked to the other side of the dais, taking Gar's hand. Rook joined his wife, Rose. Raven went to dance with her husband, Jonathon.

"I miss Robin," said Sage, seeming lonely. "I wish he were here to dance with me right now."

"I'll stay with you so you won't be by yourself." Martine had just turned around to pick up her wine when she saw the piercing eyes of David staring up at her from the foot of the dais table. Since he was on the ground level and she was on a raised platform, she looked down at him just like the nobles always did to commoners.

"Lady Martine," said David, pushing back a lock of hair. "I wondered if I could speak with you, please."

"Well, I don't know," she answered, trying to sound nonchalant, wanting to make him sweat. She toyed with him and she didn't care. Slowly, Martine picked up her goblet, taking a sip of wine. She had to hold back her smile when she saw David nervously shifting his weight from one foot to the other and wringing his hands together. Putting down her goblet, she decided to grant his request, but didn't have the chance to let him know. Lord Gar walked up to the front of the dais with another knight.

"Lady Martine, this is Sir Emery," said Gar with a nod to the other man.

"What?" she asked, not wanting to be interrupted. "Hello, Sir Emery. It's nice to meet you," she said with a nod, doing so only because it was the way she was expected to act.

"I'd like this dance, my lady, if I could," said Emery. He wasn't all that good looking and was also quite a bit older than Martine. She didn't want to dance with him, she wanted to continue speaking with David.

Her eyes flashed back to David. He did a half bow to the men and backed up, heading for the door.

It took all of her resolve not to call out to him and ask him to stay. She wanted to speak with David, even though earlier she wanted him to go to hell. For some reason, she couldn't stay mad at him. He had wanted to say something to her but now she'd never find out what it was because she had to dance with a knight she didn't know and certainly didn't like.

"Of course, Sir Emery," she said with a sigh, doing what was proper. Even if David had stayed instead of leaving, she couldn't reject a nobleman to be with a commoner. It just wasn't done.

Sadly, she walked down from the dais, taking Sir Emery's hand and heading to the center of the room to dance. All she wished, more than anything, was that it was David's hand she held right now.

David stood in the corridor out of sight, watching as Martine took the nobleman's hand and began to dance. Her movements were so fluid. She held such grace and poise. Her years of training to be a lady showed. This was who she was and who she needed to be. Now he knew that he had no right even showing his face at the castle in the first place and only wished he had stayed back at the tavern. It was guilt eating at him that made him come here today. He had seen how his words had hurt Lady Martine and he wanted to apologize.

He sadly turned and left the great hall, realizing now it was never going to happen. David felt awkward being at the castle. He never wanted to come here because it felt so foreign to him. But in his heart he realized that Martine didn't deserve the lie he'd told her. He had made it sound as if their intimate time together meant nothing to him, when it really meant the world and more. He had only told her that to make her dislike him, and now he could see that it had worked.

He did care for Martine, but she would only be risking everything to be with him. He didn't want that for her. She deserved so much more. She deserved the life of a lady with wealth and respect and things that he could never give her. Their kisses were special to him, but now, she'd never know his true feelings. Because of his own doings, the relationship between them was truly over. David could never step foot in such an elegant place as the castle ever again.

CHAPTER 8

It had been a week now since David saw Martine at Blake Castle. Every time the door to the tavern opened, his gaze shot across the room hoping to see her walking back into his life. But she didn't. What the hell had he done? He'd let his last chance slip through his fingers to tell her how he really felt about her. The pain was too much. He did everything he could to stay busy to keep his thoughts off of the lady he fancied and would never kiss again.

"David, do you want me?"

He felt an arm slip around his waist as he served men ale and whisky at the drink board.

"Cinnamon, get to work," he said, not even stopping to look back at the whore.

"That's what I'm trying to do." She pressed her body up tight to him while one hand slipped down the front of his breeches. She tried to get a rise out of him. At other times this might have worked, but not today.

"Stop it," he said, pushing her hand away. "I'm not

interested." He picked up a few dirty cups and dunked them into a bucket of water to clean them.

"You used to be interested, David. What's changed with you?" Cinnamon pouted and continued to touch him.

The door to the tavern opened and the room suddenly became quiet. That could only mean that nobles had entered his establishment. He looked up to see a crowd of people gathered around the door. Cocking his head, he tried to see who had entered. Then he noticed the jet-black hair of Lady Raven. No one could miss the sword she carried at her side either. This was Lord Corbett Blake's only daughter. A daughter who fought as well as any man.

"David, they're here to collect the rent," shouted Dirk from across the room, making David cringe. Dirk had a big mouth. David didn't want all his patrons knowing his business or his problems.

"Get back to work," he told the whore, stepping around her and hurrying over to tell Lady Raven the bad news that he couldn't pay. "I'm sorry, my lady, but I don't–" He stopped speaking as he pushed through the crowd and saw Lady Martine standing next to her cousin. He hadn't expected this. It made his heart race.

"I'm here for the rent," said Raven, taking a ledger that her guard handed her. She opened it to a page and scanned down it with the tip of her finger. "It seems you are delinquent by four months. That's not good. Not good at all. Do you have the money owed?"

"Can we please speak about this in private, my lady?" asked David, noticing everyone staring and listening.

"Go into the kitchen. It's quieter in there," instructed Uncle Joe from his chair at the entrance.

"Nay, here is fine. I'm in a hurry," said Raven. "I have a lot of stops to make today. Now do you have the money or not? My father has written here that he's allowed you extra time but will not do so again. Therefore, if you cannot pay all that you owe, my father has instructed me to close down your business and take it from you." There were surprised and concerned mumbles from the commoners who had heard this.

"Please, if we could just talk in the kitchen," begged David, wanting to try to barter for more time. But Lady Raven was stubborn. He didn't think she'd give him another chance. Not after her father wrote right in the ledger that no more chances would be given. However, Martine was with her. Hopefully, she would help. David looked over at Martine in a form of silent pleading to convince her cousin to let his family keep the inn.

"Raven, I will handle this. Why don't you move on to the next stop so we can finish soon?" said Martine.

"And leave you here unguarded?" Raven made a face. "Nay, I can't do that."

"I assure you, Lady Martine will be safe," interjected David, really wanting Raven to leave. "She'll be in my care until your return. I promise you that no harm will come to her."

"His family has already proven their worth when they took us in from the storm and helped Sage with birthing her baby," Martine reminded her cousin. "I'll be fine, Raven. Continue collecting the rents and then stop back to get me on your return to the castle."

"Are you sure about this?" asked Raven, looking first at

Martine and then over to David and then back to Martine again.

"I'm sure. Trust me. I will handle this," she told Raven.

"It's against my better judgment, but I have no time to waste today. Besides, I'm not feeling well." Her hand went to her belly. "I'll go, but I'm leaving the guard with you."

"Raven, you have the money box, not to mention you are feeling ill. It would be wiser if the guard went with you instead," said Martine.

"I'll help protect Lady Martine." Dirk walked up and crossed his arms over his sturdy chest. "You have our word she will be safe, my lady."

David realized Dirk was helping him when his cousin looked over and winked, silently saying he knew David had feelings for the girl.

"Go on," Martine told Raven with a jerk of her hand. "I'll be fine. We both have work to do."

"Well, I guess it will be all right." Raven looked at one man and then the other. Then, she shocked them all when she drew her blade and held the tip out, pointing directly at David and his cousin. Both he and Dirk jumped back, not wanting to get hit. "I warn you, if a single hair on Lady Martine's head is harmed, I promise you I'll lop off both of your heads without even blinking an eye or asking questions. Do you understand?"

Both the men silently nodded.

"Good." Raven sheathed her sword and turned and left the tavern with the guard dogging her heels.

"God's eyes, she's a mean one," said Dirk, rubbing his throat and swallowing forcefully. He still had a horrified look on his face.

"She's not normally that nasty," said Martine with a smile. "It's just that she's pregnant and emotional. So be sure not to anger her."

"I'll try hard to remember that," mumbled Dirk, heading back to his place at the door.

"I don't have the money," David told Martine in a soft voice as soon as the crowd had dissipated and went back to drinking and talking again.

"I know," she answered, kindness in her tone. "Is there somewhere we can talk? Alone," she said, glancing over at Dirk who was watching them and Uncle Joe who was listening with his head cocked.

"This is a tavern, my lady. It's far from private," David reminded her. "However, I suppose we can use my family's living quarters. No one will be in there at this time. Unless, of course, if that is too improper for a lady to be in the room alone with me and unchaperoned."

"Go," she told him with a nod of her head. "And don't worry about what's improper. I'll let you know."

David led her to his family's chamber, opening the door and letting her enter the room first. He followed her inside, lighting a candle and closing the door behind them.

"We can talk privately in here," he told her.

"Good," she said, taking off her cloak and handing it to him.

"What are you doing?" he asked, already feeling uncomfortable since they were alone and she was already taking off clothes. His eyes darted over to the door as he took her cloak from her.

"I just want to be comfortable. Is there somewhere I can sit?" She turned to look at the room.

David quickly hung up her cloak on a hook on the wall. "There is nowhere to sit in this room except for the beds, but that wouldn't be advisable." He turned around to see her sitting on his new bed, leaning back on her elbows and swinging her feet back and forth. Definitely not proper at all.

"This is nice. Don't you agree?" she asked in a cheery tone.

He wasn't quite sure how to answer. After all, a lady sitting on his bed was fine indeed. Still, he didn't think that's what she meant and was afraid to ask her to explain her comment.

"I appreciate the gift of the new bed. I've been meaning to tell you." David tried to change the subject.

"It was the least we could do since you graciously gave up your pallet to Sage the last time we were here."

He hadn't graciously given up anything for them. It was more like he was told he had to do it. However, right now David didn't want to point that out. If he did, it would only make him sound heartless.

"I suppose you're going to take the inn away from me now that I can't pay," he said, not one for small talk and wanting to get right to the point.

"Before we talk about the inn or the rent, I need to ask you something." She stood up and walked over to join him. "Why did you come to eat at the castle after you'd already told me you wouldn't be there?"

"I guess I had a change of mind."

"About the meal? Or about me?" she asked boldly, obviously liking to get right to the point as well.

"Lady Martine, I have to admit that I wasn't exactly honest with you the last time you were here."

"How so?"

"I was angry and acting harsh when that was not at all the way I wanted to be. I came to the castle because I needed to explain that to you. I realized you might have gotten the wrong opinion of me. But I suppose it no longer matters."

"What in the devil's name is that supposed to mean?" She looked at him like he had two heads.

"Martine. I mean, Lady Martine, the kisses we shared did mean something to me even if I told you they didn't. You see, I do have feelings for you even though I didn't want to admit it."

"Really." Her voice became soft and gentle. If he wasn't mistaken, she almost looked pleased. The corners of her mouth turned up slightly. "Why didn't you want me to know?" Now pain showed in her eyes, mixed with curiosity.

"I guess it was because I know where I stand as a commoner, and it's surely not with a noble. I had no right to kiss you let alone touch you. I'm not sure what the hell I was thinking. I'm sorry."

"You're sorry?" This seemed to confuse her instead of please her. "Don't you like being with me?" she asked him.

"More than you know."

"I see." She crossed her arms and paced the room, seeming to be in thought. "I am a noble and you are a commoner. I suppose that makes a big barrier between us."

"Yes. A huge barrier, my lady. We are from two different worlds and always will be. So you do understand what I mean then." He felt relieved. That is, until he heard what she had to say next.

"So, you can't pay the four months late rent?"

Suddenly, they were back to business again. Just as he had started thinking she wanted to talk about them, she pushed any emotion aside. This woman was confusing him to no end.

"You know I can't pay. I already told you that. Please. Just give me more time. I'm sure I can somehow raise the money."

"Time?" She stopped pacing and looked directly at him. "Nay, I'm sorry but I can't do that. Uncle Corbett would be furious with that decision. You didn't hold up your end of the agreement. It wouldn't be fair to just let it go, would it?"

"Mayhap not, but surely there must be something you can do to help me."

"Why should I? Because of our situation, you think you deserve special favors?" That cut him to the bone. Is that really why she thought he'd kissed her?

"Nay. Of course not. Asking for more time has nothing to do with our feelings for each other."

"I'm sorry, David, but if you can't pay what you owe then I will have to take the inn from you as was agreed upon when you signed the contract. It is the deal you made with my uncle. He owns this land and you agreed to pay rent to have your business here. You've broken that promise."

"Not really. You see, my father made that deal with Lord Corbett, not me."

"Your father is dead is he not?"

"Yes." David released a deep breath and looked to the floor, missing the man immensely. "His heart gave out about a year ago."

"Now you hold the position of proprietor and are responsible for making the payments."

"Aye. Yes, of course. You know that."

She held out her hand. "Then the deed, please."

David blinked in shock, not expecting this when she said she wanted to speak in private. My, how cold she'd turned so quickly. This was a side of Martine that he'd never seen and didn't like at all.

"Martine, nay." Panic rushed through him. How could she turn him away after he asked for her help? Mayhap he really didn't know the woman because he thought she'd be kind. Not mean like her cousin. "You're not really going to take away my family's business, are you? This is our home. We'll have nowhere to live. Nowhere to go." He wanted to shout out in anger and tell her not to do it. Not after his family had bent over backwards to help them. His family didn't deserve to be homeless. He didn't want to lose everything to a noble just because he wasn't rich enough to pay the enormous rent demanded of him. "It's not fair."

There was a moment of silence between them. He'd given it a try and it hadn't worked. Why had he even hoped that it would?

"I have a job to do, David, and I'm here to do it."

"You're right," he finally said with a sigh, walking over and opening the lid of a wooden box. "Here is the deed." He picked it up reverently since this was everything his family had worked so hard for all of their lives. "I'll sign it over to Lord Blake as agreed upon." He picked up a quill.

"Nay, wait," she said, surprising him once again.

"My lady?" he asked in question, turning around while holding his breath, hoping she'd had a change of heart.

"Sign it over to me instead, not my uncle."

"To... ?" He stared at her in confusion. The mean streak he'd seen in Lady Raven was now rearing its ugly head in her once again. He supposed it was in their blood and they couldn't help it. After all, why would they even care about poor commoners like David and his family? They were nobles and thought differently than the townsfolk. They didn't know what it was to go hungry or to worry they'd have nowhere at night to lay their heads.

"Your tavern and your inn will be mine now," she announced proudly with her chin held high in the air."

"Yes, my lady." He solemnly turned to basically sign his life over to her.

"However, I'll give you the benefit of the doubt."

He quickly signed the paper and looked back over his shoulder at her. "What does that mean?"

"I mean, I'll give you the time requested. A little time, but not much."

"I'd appreciate any time at all."

"If you can pay all the rent owed before my uncle returns, I'll sign the establishment back over to you."

"When will Lord Corbett return?" he wondered, hoping for more time than less.

"I have no idea. However, my guess is that it'll be soon."

"You know I can't do it too quickly. These things take time. Besides, I still need to come up with a plan on how to raise the funds."

"I must admit that I am good at a lot of things you probably would never suspect, David. I am going to help you earn that money."

"My lady!" he gasped. "Please, I would never want you to compromise yourself in such a manner."

"In what manner?" she asked. Then her eyes popped open wide. "Oh, no! That's not what I meant. I would never–"

"Of course not." He held up a hand, partially to cover the shame on his face. "I knew that," he said, feeling a sense of relief that she wasn't suggesting she'd whore herself out. He felt very embarrassed for even thinking that was what she meant in the first place. He supposed his mind was still on Cinnamon and the games she'd played with him earlier.

There was a knock on the door to the room, taking their attention. Then before they could even respond, the door squeaked opened and Raven stepped inside.

"Martine? What are you doing in here alone with this man?" asked Raven, not looking pleased at all.

"Why are you here?" Martine asked her cousin in return. "I thought you went out to collect the rents. I told you, I'd handle this."

"I did go, but I came back. My stomach is too upset to conduct business today. I've decided to go back to the castle." Raven's hand went to her belly. "I think it might have something to do with being pregnant."

"Did you want me to finish collecting the rents in town for you?" asked Martine.

"Don't bother. I'll have Rook finish up tomorrow. Are you ready to leave?"

"Not yet," said Martine, taking the signed deed from David.

"Oh, I see you took back the inn. Good. That's what Father would have done if he were here. I didn't really think this man would be able to pay," said Raven, scrutinizing David. "I'll tell the guard to make the customers leave and we'll put a sign on the door that it's closed for good. When Father returns he'll find another renter."

"Nay, you can't do that." Martine handed the papers to Raven. "You see, the inn already has a new owner."

"Yes. My father," said Raven.

"Nay, it's not Uncle Corbett. Look closely at the paper," said Martine, motioning to the parchment in Raven's hand.

Raven read it and her eyes popped open wide in surprise. "You took ownership of the inn?"

"Yes," said Martine.

"But why?"

"Because the Stone family helped our family and I would like to do the same in return."

"This doesn't make sense," said Raven. "You are a lady and know nothing about running a tavern or inn and neither should you. It's not proper."

"I don't see anything wrong with it," replied Martine nonchalantly. "It is a challenge. I, like you, enjoy to be challenged."

"I don't understand." Raven furrowed her brow and shook her head. "What on earth are you planning to do? If you give them money to pay their debts, it'll go against the contract. You can't do that."

"I am not giving them anything but my assistance," she told her cousin. "You see, I am going to return to the inn every day for a while to help David and his family with the business."

"Here?" gasped David and Raven together.

"Yes, here." Martine was sure of this and wasn't going to

let anyone intimidate her or sway her decision. "I am good at running the household back home. My mother trained me. I know all about keeping ledgers and taking inventory and what to do to make certain things run smoothly. It can't be that different."

"Nay, my lady. You can't do this," said David.

"Why not?" asked Martine. "Don't you think I'm capable?" Her hands went to her hips.

"I am sure you are quite capable. I just meant, because you're a noble," David answered.

"I'm well aware of my status, thank you. Don't let it bother you because I'm not going to let it stop me."

"Nay, Martine. David is right," agreed Raven. "You can't be working alongside commoners. What will people think? Your place is at the castle." Raven still rubbed her aching belly.

"Raven, for heaven's sake, don't give me a hard time about this," spat Martine. "I've made my decision. I want to do it. Besides, it's not like I plan on waiting tables. There are other ways I can help the Stone family. And it's only for a short while."

"I still don't like it," snapped Raven. "Neither will my brother or my father once they hear about this."

"What is there not to like?" Martine wanted to know. "I'm only here to help them get back on their feet. Why are you so upset? For goodness sake, it's not like I'm telling you I'm going to marry the man."

"Marry?" mumbled David, his head going back and forth as the women quarreled. Just the word put a knot in his stomach. This is something he'd been avoiding for quite some time now. He wasn't at all in a hurry to marry anyone.

"I sure hope you won't marry a mere innkeeper," remarked Raven. "That'll make your father as well as mine furious. Don't do that to them."

"I don't know why you'd even say that to me, Raven," continued Martine. "I mean, after all, you married a black-smith and Rook married a gardener. So if I wanted to marry a commoner too, what's the difference? Try to be a little more understanding about my situation."

"Father would never agree with this crazy idea of you helping them. A tavern is not where a lady should be."

Martine swished her hand through the air. "Uncle Corbett is not here to object. And by the time he returns I am sure David and his family will be back on their feet again. So, you see, it is nothing to worry about at all," stated Martine.

"Well, what about your mother? Or mine for that matter? What will they think?" asked Raven, her face starting to turn a pale shade of green. "Oh, Martine, I really don't feel well." Raven grimaced and bent over slightly.

"Raven, you're pregnant and should be back at the castle with your feet propped up in the ladies solar. I'll go back with you now and finalize things with Lady Devon. You don't need to concern yourself with any of this." Martine turned back to talk with David. "Relay the message to your family that I will return here tomorrow. We'll have to work hard to raise the rent money before the knights return, so I suggest we get started immediately."

"Thank you, my lady, but are you sure about this?" asked David, not able to see how this was going to work even though he appreciated her offer. "I don't understand what you're actually going to do here at the inn."

"We'll figure something out," she told him.

"Martine, I really need to leave. Right now," Raven told her. "I feel as if I'm going to vomit."

"My cloak. Quickly," Martine held out her arm to David.

He ran and got it and helped her don it.

"I need to take my cousin back to the castle, but expect me here bright and early in the morning," said Martine, taking the deed to the inn and leaving.

David's mother and sisters walked in as the nobles walked out. His family curtsied and didn't say a word until the ladies had left.

"David? What's going on here?" asked Greta.

"I saw you enter the room with Lady Martine," said Matilda with wide eyes. "Brother, what were you thinking? Why were you in here alone with her?"

"I was giving her something she wanted." As soon as David said the words he realized how improper that sounded. "I mean we were conducting business."

"In the bedroom?" Cecelia gasped. "Oh, David, what did you do?"

"Nay! Stop it." He held up a halting hand to his sisters. "That's not what I meant at all and you know it."

"No, we don't know it," said Cecelia. "The door was closed and no one knows what went on in here."

"David? What did you give her?" asked Greta curiously, coming to his side.

"Mother, we are four months late with the rent," he told her.

"Oh, no." His mother's hand went to her mouth. "Why didn't you say something about this sooner? I had no idea it was so bad."

David put his arm around his mother's shoulders. "I didn't tell any of you because I didn't want you to worry."

"Well, we're certainly worried now," said Matilda in a sharp tone. "David, you should have told us."

"Then did Lord Corbett take the inn away from us? Did we lose our home?" The fear on Cecelia's face said it all. The poor girl lost her husband a few months ago and was about to birth a baby soon and would have to raise it on her own. David had to say something, anything, to try to comfort her.

"Nay, Lord Corbett didn't take it," he said, which was the truth.

"Oh, good," said Greta. "I'd hate to think we lost the inn."

David cleared his throat.

"There's more, isn't there?" asked Matilda.

"Yes," said David. "Since we didn't have the rent money, I had to give up the inn after all, but we won't be forced to leave here."

"That makes no sense," said Uncle Joe from the door. He and Dirk had been standing there listening and David hadn't even known it. "If we lost the inn then why are they letting us stay here?"

"Because we have a new owner now," explained David.

"A new owner? Who?" Dirk wanted to know.

David released a deep breath and answered. "Lady Martine now owns the Cross Hare Inn. She left for now but will be back tomorrow. She's going to help us raise the money to pay off our debts. The only thing is, we need to do it before her father and uncle return."

"That makes no sense," spat Dirk.

Uncle Joe spoke up next. "Do you mean we have only

until Lord Corbett returns to try to earn the money, or we really will lose the inn and have no place to live?"

"Yes. I suppose that is exactly what I'm trying to say," David answered.

"When will he return?" asked Matilda.

"We don't know the answer to that." This wasn't getting any easier for David.

"In other words, it might be a month or two or it could only be a day or two?" asked his mother.

"Mayhap," said David with a shrug. "It's a chance we'll have to take. We have no other choice. Lady Martine is trying to help us."

The room was silent and no one said a word.

Finally, Dirk spoke up. "Since Lady Martine is going to be here and our living quarters are small, I volunteer to share my bed with her," he said, making the girls giggle and causing David to want to slug him.

"She's not staying here at night," David told them. "At least, I don't think so. Either way, you're not sharing a bed with a noblewoman so get that crazy idea out of your head right now."

"David is right." Joe used his cane to tap the floor and stepped forward. "We don't have another choice. We should be thankful Lady Martine wants to help us. I don't believe any other noble would be so accommodating in our situation."

"I agree," spoke up his mother. "I like Lady Martine."

"So do we," Cecelia answered for her and Matilda. "We'll do anything she says if it'll help us save our home."

"Me too," said David softly, walking over and closing the lid on the empty wooden box that had held the deed to the inn. He was the head of this family now and it was up to him to make sure things went smoothly. Especially, when Lady Martine returned. Even though he wasn't sure how having Martine here was going to work or what she could actually do to help them, it at least gave his family hope. As disturbing as this whole situation was, at the same time David still had a good feeling deep down. Martine wasn't a shrew after all. This proved she still had a good heart.

One good thing that came from all of this was that now he'd have a real reason to be close to Lady Martine. With any luck, mayhap he'd even get another chance to kiss her.

CHAPTER 9

"Let me get this straight," said Lady Devon the next morning as she, Sage, Josefina, and Martine sat sewing in the ladies solar. Raven was there as well, still feeling ill. She didn't usually sew but was trying to learn the skill since she'd soon be a mother. "Martine, you took ownership of the Cross Hare Inn?"

"Father's not going to like that," said Raven, squinting and trying to thread a needle.

"Nay, I don't suppose Corbett will," said Devon, not sounding too concerned.

"I only did it so the Stone family wouldn't lose their home," explained Martine. "I'm going to help them earn the rent money. By the time my father and Uncle Corbett return, I'm sure David will be caught up with the rent and I'll hand him back the deed."

"Why would you even do such a thing?" asked Devon.

"Because, they helped us. Especially Sage. I'm just

returning the favor." Martine saw the smiles on Josefina and Sage's faces and knew they were going to spill her secret.

"She's sweet on the boy named David," said Josefina.

"He's a man, not a boy," Martine corrected her. "And I'm not sweet on him. Not really." She couldn't even look at the others. Neither could she focus on her sewing.

"God's teeth, Martine! I had no idea you had feelings for that innkeeper," said Raven. "It all makes sense now why you did what you did."

"We knew about it all along," said Sage with a giggle.

"Why am I always the last to know?" Raven gave up trying to thread the needle, tossing it into her sewing basket and then proceeding to retch into the basket afterwards. "Ooooooh, why am I so ill? Sage, did you feel like this when you were pregnant?"

"Nay, not at all," said Sage sounding much too cheery for so early in the morning. "I have some herbs that will help you." Sage put down her sewing and got up. "Come with me." She held out her hand. "We'll get the herbs and then go check in with the nursemaid to see little Martin. I miss him."

"You spent all morning with the baby," said Josefina. "Let the nursemaid take him for a while so you can rest."

"I have more energy when I'm around my baby," protested Sage. "You'll all see what I mean as soon as you have children of your own."

"I agree," said Devon, focusing on her stitching. "Being a mother is a wonderful thing."

Once Sage and Raven left the room, Devon brought up the subject again of the inn. "Martine, won't it be tiring traveling back and forth to the inn every day?"

"Not really," said Martine, putting down her sewing. "It's not that far away. If it's bad weather, I'll just... stay there overnight, I guess."

"What?" Josefina gasped, pricking herself with a needle. "Ouch," she said, bringing her finger to her mouth. "I'm not good at this." She put down the basket. Josefina was a merchant by trade and she and Sage and Rose had been trying their hardest to learn the skills of a noblewoman now that they were married to lords. "Martine, you can't stay at the inn with David. It's not right or proper."

"Not right? Not proper?" asked Martine, blowing air from her mouth. "Unless you are forgetting, I stayed on the ship with you and a bunch of men when you traveled to trade shows to sell your wares." Martine spoke of the journey she took recently with Josefina and Gar. "If anything isn't right, I'd say it has to be that."

"That's different. Robin was there to protect you and so was Gar," Josefina reminded her. "And don't forget, I wasn't a noblewoman at the time. I was just a merchant who hired Gar to sail my ship for me."

"Everyone is worrying too much," interrupted Devon. "You are mature women and can make decisions for yourself. Even if the men won't agree with it, I support you." Devon had caused Corbett a lot of trouble in the past. It was at a time when she was his servant, before she discovered that she was noble.

"Thank you, Lady Devon," said Martine. "I am sure there is nothing for anyone to worry about. I will be fine. I'll just be in town, not on a stormy ocean. It's safe, I tell you. Besides, David will be there to protect me."

"Oh, does David have skill with weapons?" asked Devon curiously, making Martine wish she hadn't asked that question.

"I don't think David even owns a weapon besides his eating knife," blurted out Josefina. "Or at least, I didn't see any weapons when we were there."

"That doesn't matter." Martine tried hard to convince the others as well as herself. "I'm sure he knows how to fight. After all, I saw him and his cousin Dirk throw men out of the tavern on their ear. With force," she added, rubbing her arm, remembering being knocked down when one of the men being tossed out knocked into her.

"It sounds like you've already made up your mind, my dear," said Devon. "Therefore, there is no need to discuss this any further." She held up a baby's garment she was sewing and smiled.

"Does that mean you're not going to stop me?" asked Martine, astonished that this was going so smoothly.

"Did you want me to stop you?" Devon lowered the baby clothes and looked over at Martine.

"Nay. Of course not."

"Then I won't."

"Mayhap it'll be a good time for you to get to know David," said Josefina, picking up her sewing once again to inspect it. "That is, before your father and uncle return, I mean."

"I know they won't be happy about it, but I really like David. I would like to know him better," said Martine. "Even if he is a commoner."

"It won't be the first time this family has married from

below the salt and I'm sure it won't be the last," said Devon with a wry smile.

"Wait a minute. Stop right there," said Martine. "I never said anything about marrying the man."

"Nay, you didn't, but you didn't need to," said Devon with a kind smile. "I see it in your eyes, Martine. You long to find true love just like your brother and cousins have done. I was that way once too. It's part of being a woman, I guess."

"What do you mean?" asked Martine.

"I mean, most women deep down feel a need to find the right man, and also to have children. It's very important to them."

"I'm not sure Raven would agree with that right now," said Josefina. "She seems miserable being pregnant."

"She won't be ill for long, I'm sure," Devon answered. "Please, don't let her gruff exterior fool you. Raven wants children just as much as the next woman."

"If you don't mind, I'll be going now," said Martine, standing up and brushing off her gown.

"At least let a guard escort you to and from the inn," said Devon. "I insist."

"If it makes you feel better, I'll agree," said Martine. "However, I don't want Dexter or any of the guards staying at the inn while I'm there."

"I understand," said Devon. "Having time alone with David will be important. You won't be able to get that private time with a guard watching over your shoulder, will you? Have fun!"

"Thank you," said Martine, feeling as though her aunt really understood her. Then another thought popped into her head. She wasn't sure everyone would be as understanding about this as Lady Devon. Stopping at the door, she turned around. "Aunt Devon, do you think you can possibly mention this to my mother?"

"You can send her a missive the same as I can," said Devon, continuing to sew.

"True. But if she knows you agree with my plan, she'll be more apt not to fight it."

"I'll do what I can," said Devon. "Now, go. David is waiting."

David was up early the next morning, pouring over the ledgers, trying his best to find out where he went wrong. He was sure they'd been bringing in enough money to cover the rent and still have enough left for food, wine and ale as well. By his calculations, it was tight, but he should still have had money to pay the rent. The only thing is, every month when he counted the money in the box, they came up short.

"There has to be something I'm missing," he muttered to himself. Mayhap having another pair of eyes on things would be good, he decided. However, having Martine there was only going to prove distracting.

"Is the girl here yet?" Uncle Joe walked to the drink board, using his cane and touching each table and chair. Since he was blind, David hadn't been able to move the tables or benches around. It took Uncle Joe a long time to be able to get around without his sight. Now he knew where everything was and it gave him the freedom he longed for.

"Nay, she's not here yet, Uncle Joe."

"Mayhap she's not coming." Dirk followed Joe from the kitchen, chomping on a small loaf of bread that he'd most likely swiped from the cook.

"If Lady Martine said she'll be here, she will," David told them. "Dirk, stop eating all the profits. That bread is for the paying customers. Our family eats the leftovers."

"I'm hungry and there are no leftovers yet," said the big man who never seemed to stop eating. "Besides, this is yesterday's bread. It's already stale."

"We use the stale bread for trenchers when we run out of bowls and plates and you know it. It makes a good container to serve the pottage in. The customers like gnawing on the bread afterwards." David's attention was on the books again.

"You never smile anymore, David," said Uncle Joe, taking a seat at a table across from the drink board.

"I don't smile?" David asked. "Uncle Joe, not to be rude, but how would you know?"

"I don't need eyes to see it," explained the blind man. "I can hear smiles in people's words. In their voices. Your father used to be happy and smile a lot. That is, until he let the business end up worrying him to death."

"Father died from a bad heart, not from worrying," said David, picking up a cup of ale and taking a swig.

"You'll die from not knowing how to relax," continued Uncle Joe. "You are following in your father's footsteps."

"Mayhap I am, but it is my job to do so now that Father is gone."

"You have another responsibility as well."

"What are you suggesting?" asked David. "That I take the day off when we've already lost our inn and I'm trying desperately to get it back? Because if so, I'd never do that."

"Neither did your father," Uncle Joe mumbled under his breath.

"Where's Mother?" asked David, looking around the room. "I didn't see her in the living quarters this morning and neither was she in the kitchen."

"She's gone. She left early this morning for the alehouse," Joe told him. "Cecelia went with her. We're low on wine and ale and might not even have enough to make it through the night."

"What?" David's head snapped upward. "Already?"

"It was that crowd we had on the stormy night," said Dirk, talking as he chewed with his mouth open. "They drank a lot."

"For drinking so much, I don't see enough coin here." David ran his hand through the coins in the money box, the metal pieces clicking together.

"Dirk gave away a lot of drinks that night," Joe told him.

"I had to!" Dirk finished chewing and swallowed. "The customers were angry and I had to appease them so they wouldn't fight. You know how everything gets busted when fights break out."

"I suppose that was a good idea," answered David. "Fighting would only ruin more of our belongings and that would cost more to replace in the long run."

"I'm sure the girls will be back soon," said Joe.

David looked up from his work. "I don't want Cecelia hauling those heavy barrels. She's pregnant! We don't want her to go into labor early and have another situation on our hands like we did with Lady Sage."

"Nay, no one wants that," agreed Dirk.

"Cecelia and Mother can't load the cart by themselves. Why didn't you go with them to help, Dirk?"

"Didn't know they were going." Dirk poured himself a big cup of ale to wash down the bread he'd devoured.

"Never mind." David snapped shut the ledger and put it back behind the counter. Then he took a handful of coins from the box, putting the box and ledger back in the secret compartment behind the drink board, being sure to lock it. "I'll go to the alehouse and load the barrels myself. You two clean up the tavern and check the rooms upstairs while you're at it. Any paying guest needs to either leave before we open for business or pay for another night."

"We have no guests," said Joe. "Just one customer of Cinnamon's and he hasn't come downstairs yet."

"Then clean everything else for now. I don't want this place looking filthy when Martine arrives."

"This isn't a castle, it's a goddamn tavern, David," said Joe. "You can't expect so much out of us."

"I'll take care of Lady Martine while you're gone, don't worry," said Dirk with a loud belch.

David donned his cloak. "Tell her that I'll be back soon. Be sure not to let her leave to look for me. She's under our protection now and needs to stay here. The roads are filled with thieves and cutthroats. We've made a promise for her safety and we need to keep it."

David headed out the door and to the stables for his horse. He should have sent Dirk to the alehouse since

Martine would be there soon, but David needed to do this. Dirk wasn't good with bartering or making deals for good prices. David needed to haggle with the alewives today because what he wanted was more than just wine or ale. What he wanted was important. Not to him, but to Lady Martine.

"My lady. Enter." Dirk stood at the open door to the tavern, extending an inviting arm as Martine dismounted her horse. Dexter, the castle guard ran over to help her.

"I'm fine, Dexter. I don't need help to dismount, but thank you." Martine, much like her cousin Raven, preferred to do things for herself.

It was a cold but sunny day, almost making her forget it was winter. Excitement coursed through her because she knew David was inside. Martine couldn't wait to see him again.

"May I take your horse, my lady?" A boy ran out from the stables to collect it.

Martine wasn't sure if this was someone who worked for David, or if the boy was a thief, just pretending to stable her horse when he really planned to steal it.

"I'm not sure." She looked back to the door of the tavern and Dirk nodded.

"That's James. He's our stable boy and Cecelia's nephew. You can give him your horse and he'll watch it closely for you, my lady."

"All right, then." She gave the reins to the boy as Dexter took her travel bag off her horse. The guard planned on carrying it inside for her. Martine didn't want him in the tavern because she knew the man liked to drink. He'd most likely ask for a drink and sit there all day not leaving. There was no need for the guard to even step foot inside. The tavern wasn't open yet. Plus, she would be in good hands and didn't need his protection. "I can take it from here," she told Dexter, pulling the bag from his hold. "You are dismissed. Be back at midnight to escort me home."

"Midnight?" growled Dexter. "The roads aren't safe that time of night. I'll collect you before the sun sets."

"Nay. That will never do," she told him. "Most of the tavern's business doesn't even start until the set of the sun. If I'm going to be of any help to these people, I have to stay here later."

"I'll discuss this with Lady Devon," said Dexter mounting his horse. "Go on. Get inside before I leave, my lady."

"I'm going. Now leave. Please." She headed to the tavern. Dirk ran out and took her bag for her.

"Allow me, my lady." Dirk was more than willing to help her and smiled at her as if he thought he had a chance of getting a kiss from her like his cousin had. Dirk smelled and was sloppy. His big stomach made his tunic rise up, enabling her to see the hair on his belly. She tried not to look.

"Thank you, Dirk," she said, just to be polite, stepping into the dark tavern. She had hoped David would be there to greet her or perhaps carry her bag. He was nowhere in sight. "It is so dark in here."

"The tavern's not open yet," said Dirk. "Even though the inn part is always open."

"There's no need for firelight," came a voice from the dark. "You'll get used to the dark after a while." Martine heard a strange tapping noise across the room as well as the shuffling of feet. Then David's blind uncle walked out into the center of the room, using a cane to make sure his way was clear. He stopped in front of her. The daylight shone in from the open door, making his blind eyes look even cloudier.

"Mayhap there is no need for you to have light, Uncle Joe," said Dirk, putting the strap of Martine's bag over his shoulder as he headed to a window. "But Lady Martine isn't used to the dark like the rest of us." Dirk pulled open the shutters from one window only. Light streamed into the room.

Then came the voice of a woman. "I, for one, work better in the dark, just using my hands as a guide. And sometimes my mouth." A whore strolled down the stairs looking disheveled and with her bodice untied. Her breasts spilled out of the top, leaving little to the imagination.

"Thank you, Cinnamon. You were wonderful as usual." A man hurried down the stairs after her pulling his tunic into place. She turned around when he got to the bottom landing, grabbing his face and kissing him hard for all to see. Then Martine watched the whore run her fingers down the man's chest and to the man's groin, giving him a quick squeeze.

"Oh, you wicked little tart!" The man who looked like a villager or perhaps a traveler jumped backward when she'd grabbed his groin. "Keep that up and I'll never leave here." He dug a coin out of the pouch tied to the belt of his quickly tightening trews, and slipped the coin between the girl's breasts. "You like that?" he asked with a rotten-toothed smile, squeezing her breast, bending over like he was going to taste her.

"You know I do." Cinnamon pushed him away and removed the coin. Then once more she stroked the man, probably hoping for more money.

"That kind of behavior needs to stay behind closed doors," muttered Martine, heading over to the drink board where she thought she'd find David for sure. "Just put my bag down here," she told Dirk, nodding to a table in front of the drink board. After taking off her cloak, she looked around the room. The only ones there with her were Joe, Dirk, and the whore.

"I'll take your cloak, my lady." It was Dirk again. She really didn't want him touching her things because his hands looked filthy and his finger nails were nearly black.

"I'll keep it with me for now, thank you." She wondered if David was in back. "Actually, I'd like to hang it in your living quarters, not out here in the tavern if you don't mind. I'll do it myself." She reached for the cloak but the whore's words stopped her.

"He's not in there."

Martine stopped in mid-motion. "Who?" she asked.

Cinnamon slipped behind the drink board and poured herself a drink. "He's not in the living quarters so you don't need to bother going to look for him."

"I don't know what you're talking about." She'd been found out and she didn't like that in the least.

"You know who I mean. I'm talking about David. After all, that's why you're here, aren't you? To see him again?"

"I'm here to– never mind," she said, not feeling the need to explain herself to the tart. "Dirk, where is David?"

"Not here, like Cinnamon said." Dirk went over to the drink board to flirt with the girl.

"When will he be back?" This disappointed Martine since David knew she was coming here this morning. Why in the world would he leave?

"Don't know," said Dirk, paying no attention at all to Martine. He was leaning close to the whore and staring down her cleavage. No wonder work wasn't getting done with such needless distractions.

"What about Greta and Cecelia? Are they in the kitchen?" she asked.

"Nay, they're gone too." Uncle Joe made his way over to her, taking a seat at the table. "They had to pick up a shipment from the alehouse. And before you ask, Matilda is making up the beds upstairs."

"Oh. Of course," she said, trying not to sound disheartened. She didn't like being here if David was gone. Martine suddenly felt very uncomfortable without even the women to talk to. "Well, I suppose we should get started then. No sense wasting time." She laid her cloak on the table, looking around the filthy place. "Dirk, can you start picking up the dirty dishes? It smells foul in here. We'll need to sweep, scrub the tables, and open more windows for a while to air it out."

"It's winter. It'll make the place too cold if we open more windows," said Dirk. "Then I'll have to chop more wood for the fire. Besides, I don't start chores until after breakfast." He reached out and took a strand of Cinnamon's long hair in between his fingers and brushed it over the tops of her breasts, trying to tickle her. She slapped his hand and walked away.

"Dirk, you fool. You already ate an entire loaf of bread this morning so you had your breakfast," scolded Uncle Joe. "Listen to Lady Martine."

Martine would have given Joe a job, but she wasn't sure what a blind man could do. She figured she'd wait and ask David about him.

"You're not in your usual elaborate surroundings, Missy," said Cinnamon. "Go back to the castle where you belong."

At first, Martine felt like turning and running. She truly didn't belong here. The girl was right. Then, Martine decided she wasn't going to let the hussy upset her. That would only give her power over her and Martine wasn't about to do that.

"Excuse me, Nutmeg," she said, purposely saying the girl's pet name wrong.

"It's Cinnamon. Like Sin," said the whore with a sarcastic smile.

"I don't like that name. Besides, sinning isn't a good thing," said Martine, slowly walking over to the drink board.

"It might not sound good to you, but it is very good for me," said the whore. "Sinning is what makes me lots and lots of money." She shook the pouch of coins at her side to prove her point. It looked to be nearly full.

"Is that the money you made for the week?" asked Martine, coming up next to the girl now.

"The week? Hah! This is all from one night. That's how good I am." She removed the money pouch and held it up, shaking it and jingling the coins loudly.

"I see." Martine's hand shot out. "Hand it over."

"What? Nay. You aren't touching my money." The whore scowled at her and shoved the coin pouch down her cleavage, keeping her hands over it in a protective manner.

"If you work here, then you owe half the money you make to the inn," Martine told her.

"What? Nay. I do not!" That angered the hussy to no end. "I've always kept every coin I earned. That's the deal I had with first David's father and now with him. They let me keep what I make because I bring in lots of customers."

"Those same customers are not here buying drinks if they're up in the rooms with you now, are they?" asked Martine. "This inn pays rent to Lord Corbett Blake, and you will do the same by paying rent to David from now on." She continued to hold out her hand.

"Who do you think you are? Just because you're a noble doesn't mean you can take my money." The whore screwed up her face looking like a shrew now.

"I'm the new owner of the Cross Hare Inn," stated Martine. "Now, hand over half the money or you can find another place to work. I will not let you stay without contributing your share to keep this place open."

"You can't do that."

"Yes, she can," came a voice from the door. David walked in with a small barrel propped up on his shoulder. "Dirk, help the women out of the cart and then bring in the casks," David commanded.

"Fine," grumbled Dirk, heading outside.

David put down the barrel behind the drink board and nodded to Martine. "Good morning, Lady Martine."

"Good morning, David. I missed you when I arrived,"

she said, flashing David a smile, feeling relieved that he'd finally returned.

"I'll bet she did miss you," complained Cinnamon. "And when you bed David, Missy, are you going to give half of the coin you've earn to the tavern as well?"

Before Martine could stop herself, she reached out and slapped the whore across the face. Cinnamon raised her fists as if she were going to fight back, but David rushed over and stepped in between them.

"Stop it!" shouted David. "Cinnamon, if I hear another disrespectful word toward Lady Martine, you are out of here. Do you understand?"

"Davie, you don't mean that. Not after what we've been through together." The whore pouted and started to reach out for him but he grabbed her wrist to stop her. Martine was certain she was probably meaning to grab his groin the way she had done with her last customer.

David spoke through gritted teeth, still holding her wrist. "We've been through nothing together, Cinnamon. Absolutely nothing. Do you hear me? Now apologize to Lady Martine."

"I don't want to."

"Now!" His voice was a loud, deep bellow that even made Martine jump in surprise. She wasn't expecting this out of him.

"Oh, all right. But let go of me first. You're hurting me, Davie." She twisted out of his grip, rubbing her wrist.

"Go on, then," said David, glaring at her.

"Hmmph," sniffed Cinnamon, pulling her coin pouch out of her bodice. "Sorry, my lady."

It didn't sound sincere, but Martine didn't want to start trouble by mentioning it.

"Now, give me your pouch." David held out his hand.

"Really?"

"Really."

Cinnamon sighed and opened the ties of the pouch, starting to pick out a few coins to give him. David grabbed the pouch and threw it on the drink board. The coins spilled out, showing even more than Martine had originally thought she had. My, this girl knew how to make money.

"You weren't that busy last night," said David, pushing the coins around. "Where did all this money come from?"

"David, you're not saying I'm stealing, are you?" asked the girl. "Because my customers pay me well. I swear I earned every penny."

Martine wouldn't put it past the girl to steal. Then again, Martine did witness the whore getting a man who'd already paid for her services to give her even more coin.

"You'll split your earnings with the inn from now on, just like Lady Martine said." David swept half the coins into his hand and brought a wooden box out from under the drink board, depositing them inside. "Take the rest and go to your room. I want you rested for tonight."

"I don't like this change in you, David." The whore collected the remainder of her money in her pouch and headed back to the stairs. "She's going to ruin you and also break your heart, mark my words."

There was no need to ask who she meant this time. Martine knew the whore was talking about her.

"Lady Martine, so nice to see you." Greta walked into the

tavern, hurrying over with her eldest daughter to greet Martine.

"How is Lady Sage and baby Martin?" asked Cecelia, rubbing her belly, obviously thinking about her own baby who would arrive soon.

"Everyone is fine, thank you for asking."

"I'll go help Matilda clean the rooms upstairs." Cecelia hurried upstairs.

"I'd better go make sure Farley doesn't cut the meat for the pottage into big chunks," said Greta. "We need it to last for another three days." Greta started for the kitchen but stopped and looked over at Joe still sitting at the table. "Joe, you'd better make sure Dirk gets all the barrels into the cellar."

"He knows how to do it," said Joe.

"Just go," said Greta, making Martine realize the woman was trying to let David and Martine have time alone.

"For heaven's sake, I don't know what is going on around here today," complained Joe, getting up and heading out of the tavern.

"I'm sorry about all that. Won't you please sit down?" David escorted her to a tall stool at the drink board and helped her get seated.

"I've never actually sat at the drink board before," she told him, looking back at a table. "Perhaps I should sit over there."

"This is where I conduct my business in the mornings," said David. "Now please, stay here. I have something for you."

"You do?" she asked, curious as to what he meant. Did

he have some sort of present to give her? No man had ever given her a present before.

He put the small barrel on a low shelf and looked to be tapping out some liquid into a cup but she couldn't be sure. Then, to her surprise, he plunked down a metal goblet in front of her.

"My, that is ornate," she said, admiring the goblet, running her finger along the etched designs. "I didn't know you even had something like this here."

"It's only for nobles to use. Very important ones," he said, nodding at the cup. "Take a sip. I hope you like it."

She already liked the fact he'd referred to her as an important noble and served her a drink in a metal goblet.

"All right, but where's your drink?" she asked.

"I'm not thirsty right now but you always seem to be thirsty. Please, just try it."

"What is it?" she asked, picking up the goblet by the stem.

"It's a surprise. Just try it," he said again, sounding very anxious for her to do so.

She lifted the goblet to her mouth, expecting to taste perhaps spiced white wine or mayhap heather ale. Instead, it was something she liked so much better.

"Mmm," she said, tasting the drink and licking her lips. "It's delicious. It's mead."

"Yes, it is," he answered with a smile. "Sweet mead for Lady Martine." He gently covered her hand with his. It made her heart soar.

"Where did you find this?"

"It wasn't easy. I had to barter for it, but it was well worth it."

"It's good. Really good," she told him. "Perhaps we should serve it in the tavern."

"Nay. This entire barrel of sweet mead is for you, my lady."

She giggled. "I sincerely doubt I could drink that much of it. Besides, I won't be here long enough to do so."

"You won't?" That seemed to upset him. "What if it takes a long time to recover the money I owe?"

"I'm sure it won't take as long as you think," said Martine taking another sip of her mead. "Just collecting half of Cinnamon's earnings each night will enable you to pay the overdue rent in no time. Besides, I have several ideas that are sure to bring in more funds quickly."

"Then I suppose we should get started. What do you suggest we do first, my lady?"

"Why don't you show me your ledgers?" she asked.

"You know how to do that?" He brought forth the ledger.

"I balance the ledgers at my family's castle all the time. I'm sure it's not any different here. Plus, we'll need to take inventory of all your food and drink before we put in another order. Oh, I also want to see the rooms upstairs."

"Upstairs? Oh, nay, my lady." He shook his head as if he didn't want her going up there. "That is not a place for someone like you."

"You must have rooms for nobles to stay in when they pass through, don't you?" she asked.

"Yes, but we only have one room that is close to being suitable for a noble."

"How many rooms are there in total?"

"Six."

"Six rooms and only one for nobles? Nobles pay much

more than a commoner would. I think the first thing we need to do is to fix up those rooms and get the word out. What do you charge per night for a common room?"

"Well, most of the rooms are shared by at least a half dozen people."

"How much?" she asked again.

"A penny per head. Plus, they get a hot meal and unlimited drinks with the room."

"That's no good. You'll need to charge for the food, drink, candlelight or heat. Each guest at the inn should end up paying at least four pence by the time they leave here."

"Really?" David nodded. "We've always given them food and drink and it won't go over nicely."

"Tell them it's the new rules."

"All right, I guess. Why not?"

"Tell me more about the rooms at the inn."

"Three of the rooms are used for– well, for Cinnamon's customers."

"Nay," she said, shaking her head. "That needs to change. We need to have at least two of the six rooms ready for nobles at all times. We can charge four times the price that you charge commoners for a plain room. Plus, for an extra charge we'll provide a bath for the nobles."

"A bath?" asked David sounding as if he didn't agree. "I don't have a wooden tub."

"You and Dirk will easily be able to make a tub or two out of the empty barrels from the wine. You mother and sister can sew in a soft lining so the nobles won't get splinters from the wood. I know how to sew and can teach them how to make it."

"I suppose that would be nice," said David. "I mean, no

one wants a splinter up their ass." Martine tried hard to hold back from laughing. David never seemed to stop surprising her with the things he said.

"Three of the rooms can be used for the commoners," continued Martine. "Only a simple bowl of pottage will be given to those who share the room and only one free drink each, just so we don't lose too many customers. They'll have to pay for the rest. If they want a fire on the hearth, each person in the room will have to contribute to the cost. The same goes for candles. And speaking of candles, I noticed you have beeswax ones here. Why?" She nodded to the fixture on the ceiling.

"They last longer, and it's a struggle to get Dirk up there to change them out."

"No more wax candles," she told him, opening up the ledger and flipping through the pages. "Wax is too expensive and not meant for taverns. Tallow will do just fine."

"You mean, wax tapers aren't meant for commoners, don't you, my lady?"

Martine looked up, realizing she would have to be careful with her words so she wouldn't insult him. "We need to keep the cost of supplies down, David." She thought he'd object, but he changed the subject, no longer speaking of candles.

"You realize that only leaves one room for Cinnamon and her customers. It should be sufficient but she won't like that." David's attention roamed over to the stairs. A door slammed shut upstairs and Martine was sure Cinnamon had been listening. She didn't care. It was good that the whore eavesdropped on their plans and that she heard David agreeing to them as well.

"One room is more than enough for the whore and her business. She can't have her customers tying up the rooms. Actually, I think this inn would be better off without a whore at all. Then it would bring in more families."

"You have a lot of ideas," said David. "Ones I have never thought of before. However, Cinnamon has been here for years. I'd hate to kick her out."

"Then she'll stay for now. On a trial basis only." Martine wasn't happy with the idea, but she really didn't want anyone to be homeless.

"Trial basis?" he asked.

"Yes. Just like what I'm doing here. It is only temporary."

"These plans of yours. They might just work."

"Of course, they will, David. I told you, I can help you make money. I know what nobles like and what they'll pay for. However, you need to make them want to come in here. The stench alone is offensive."

"Stench?" he asked. "What stench?"

"The smell of urine mixed with mold and spilled drinks. Why don't you use rushes on the floor to sop up the moisture and hold down the stench?"

"It is easier for Uncle Joe using his cane if we don't have anything on the floor."

"Then you'll need to wash the floor more often. At least have more handfuls of dried sage and rosemary hanging from the rafters. Far away from the candles, of course."

"If I may say, my lady, I think you will be good for the Cross Hare Inn. Some fresh blood is just what is needed."

She looked up at the mention of blood. "By the way, I saw a bloodstain on the floor near the far table."

"I know. A fight broke out there last week. I haven't been able to remove the stain."

"Then we'll have to cover it with something. Or move the table over it."

"No, no. The tables and benches have to stay. They can't be moved. If so, Uncle Joe will trip."

"Oh, I understand. David, I know what people– what families need. It is important to cater to the needs of the many, not just the few."

"I'm willing to give anything a try, I guess. As long as it keeps my family from being homeless."

"I've already sent a missive to Glasgow from the castle."

"What for?"

"I asked my cousin's great-grandfather, Old Man MacKeefe, to send over some of his famous Mountain Magic."

"Mountain Magic? That's good whisky. I've heard of it," said David. "It is coveted and not easy to come by."

"I can get it for you and at a good price too. You know, it is the best and most potent whisky in all of Scotland and England. Men will travel a far distance for it and pay good money just to try it. Plus, it will bring in more nobles. Once the word is out that you have Mountain Magic here at the Cross Hare Inn, I promise you will always be busy."

"You have a lot of good ideas. I like them," said David. "Thank you so much for taking your time to help us." He gave her hand a slight squeeze. His skin against hers felt good. She didn't stop him because she craved the touch of the handsome innkeeper.

"David, I want to thank you again for being so hospitable to me and my family in our travels."

"I would like to think I was doing a good thing, my lady,

but I have to be honest with you." His hand slipped from hers and with it went his warmth. He reached over and poured himself a drink. She noticed it was whisky. Whisky seemed to help him relax. After all, the last time when he'd kissed her, that was what he'd been drinking.

"Go on," she said, taking another sip of the delicious mead.

"I hate to admit it, but I didn't want to give you and your entourage shelter that night of the storm."

"You didn't?"

"Nay. I am ashamed of myself now. But we were over-crowded and short on help. I was anxious as it was, and the last thing I wanted in my establishment was a noblewoman having a baby."

"Oh," she said. "I guess I can understand and I cannot say I blame you. The last thing I wanted to do was to be delivering a baby that night."

That seemed to break the tension between them. David and Martine were able to speak easily to each other now. Plus, they were the only ones in the tavern since it didn't open until later. She liked that. Martine enjoyed being in the presence of David. He was nice to look at and easy to talk to. She felt as if she could let down her walls and be herself around him.

"David, can I ask you something?" Her heart beat rapidly, waiting for him to answer.

"Of course. Ask me anything, my lady."

"Do you like being around me?"

"Do you really have to ask?" He leaned in to her, putting his elbows on the drink board. Their faces were close together.

"I do have to ask," she said. "I mean, I guess I just want to know how you feel. Around me, that is. Being with me."

"Nervous, yet excited, is how I feel around you," he said in a soft voice. He reached up and pushed a stray strand of hair behind her ear. "I also feel lucky to be in your presence. I think you are the most beautiful woman I have ever met in my life."

"Really?" She smiled, looking first into his eyes and then down to her cup. Her body was heating up just being close to him. "Would you like to– to kiss me again?" Slowly, she raised her eyes to meet his. He was staring at her as if he were captivated. If he said no now, she'd know he was a liar.

"Very much so, my lady." He said the words but still didn't do anything about it.

"It's all right," she gave him the permission she thought he was waiting for.

"What's all right?"

"You can kiss me if you want to. I won't stop you."

"I want to but I'm not sure I should."

"Why not?"

"Because, once I start I might not be able to stop."

"That's a chance I'm willing to take if you are."

That was all she had to say. Cradling her hands in his, he leaned in and kissed her gently on the lips. When he did, Martine felt her heart do a flip inside her chest. She liked David's kisses. They made her feel pretty and safe and special. He pulled back, smiling at her, his face so perfect it was like a sculpture. Never had she seen such perfect skin and nice cheekbones on a man. Not a common man anyway. His hair was down to his shoulders and wavy, his brows dancing atop his ochre eyes. The most amazing thing about his face was his mouth. Not just the way he kissed but the shape of it and the way little creases formed when he smiled. To top it off, that dimple on his chin made him irresistible.

"I have to admit something to you now," she said, her voice in a mere whisper as well.

"What is it?" he asked, his face still right in front of hers.

"I was happy to take your inn from you."

He frowned and pulled back a little. "You were?"

"Yes," she said with a nod. "I knew if I owned this inn I would be able to be with you whenever I wanted."

"Pardon me, my lady, for saying that you could do that even without taking away my business."

"Nay, I couldn't," she told him. "But now I have a reason to be here. This was the best way I could think of to see you again."

This time he boldly leaned forward and kissed her hard and long. Just the taste of his essence on her tongue made her want to bask in his pleasures and do so much more. She felt as if she were falling fast for David Stone and wasn't really even sure why. Could it be as Lady Devon said? Was it just Martine being a woman and wanting to find true love with a man the way her cousins Raven, Lark, and Eleanor had? Or was it because after seeing baby Martin, she wanted a child of her own? Mayhap it was all those things, but she felt it was so much more. It was because she found a man who cared about her and seemed to value her opinion. Noblemen usually thought a lady was only good for birthing him heirs. Never would a nobleman even listen to a one of Martine's ideas. David liked her ideas and was eager to try them. He made her feel special.

Mayhap she was moving too fast, but part of her really didn't care. She would get to know David Stone better in the time she spent here now that she was owner of the inn. Then again, she didn't need more time because she already knew he was the one she wanted. Hopefully, he felt the same way about her. She supposed the next few days or weeks or however long she'd be here would give her the answers she needed.

CHAPTER 10

I t had been a week now since Martine started making
changes at the inn. Already, the business seemed to
have picked up and for that she was happy. She had got here
early today, wanting to look back at the ledgers and to also
take inventory of what food and drink was kept at the inn.

Martine didn't see the stable boy James anywhere, and
decided he was probably asleep in the barn. Dexter yawned
atop his horse, not bothering to get off his steed anymore
when he dropped her off here.

"Where is the stable boy?" asked the guard.

"I'm sure James is just still sleeping. I'll take my horse to
him in the stables."

"I'll go with you."

"No need," she said, holding up her hand. "I actually
think I see him coming now."

"Anything else, my lady?" asked the guard with another
yawn. The sun wasn't even up yet, and it was dark but lit by

the moon. She hadn't really seen James, but she wanted Dexter to leave.

"That'll be all. You're dismissed," she told him, watching him go before she even got to the stable. Instead, she tied the reins of her horse to the hitching post just outside the tavern. She felt as if she were being watched, spinning around to find a dog sitting at her feet. "Why hello there," she said to the dog. "You're cute."

She bent over and pet the dog on the head. It was a brown mutt with matted fur. He looked as if he'd been sleeping in the barn since stalks of straw were clinging to him. The dog looked up at her with sad eyes, laying down and putting his nose between his paws. She saw his body shaking.

"You look cold and hungry," she said, digging into her travel bag slung over her shoulder. "I have something you might like." She pulled out a piece of dried beef that she'd taken from the kitchen at the castle, wanting to suggest to David that this could be used at his inn, being able to keep for a long time. All he had to do was to throw it in soup or a bubbling pot of stew for a while and it would add sustenance and also flavor since it was salted. "You can have this. You need it more than me." She held out the dried beef and the dog sprang to his feet and gobbled it down. "I'll bet you're a stray. You'll need water, too. Come, we'll get some from the night kettle in the kitchen."

She headed to the tavern and the dog followed on her heels. When she opened the door and looked inside, she realized no one was there. She supposed everyone was still sleeping and didn't want to wake them. "Come," she said, patting her leg, trying to coax the dog inside, but the animal stopped at the door and wouldn't enter.

The poor thing seemed frightened. He probably had always been an outside dog and had never stepped inside a building before and didn't know what to expect. She dug back into her bag and this time pulled out a hunk of bread. Breaking it in pieces, she dropped a trail of food, and the dog followed the tidbits inside, eating the scraps she threw down.

"There, that's better," she said in a whisper, closing the door. "You don't look so cold now."

After taking the dog to the kitchen and giving him a big drink of water, she decided to get some things done while she waited for everyone to wake up. She always rose early at the castle. Since the tavern was opened late, she supposed everyone was tired and that is why they were still sleeping. She hadn't told anyone she'd be here early today, so didn't expect to be greeted.

"Is someone out here?" David walked out into the tavern, rubbing his eyes. There was only a small tallow candle encased in a glass burning on the edge of the drink board, so the place was still dark.

"It's just me, David," she said, walking over to greet him. She stood on her tiptoes and gave him a quick kiss.

This past week at the tavern had gone smoothly. Working side by side, Martine and David had already managed to make some good changes. The tavern didn't stink anymore, and everyone was getting along. Martine had mentioned to David that Dirk smelled like sweat. When word got back to Greta, she made not only Dirk but every one of them bathe in one of the new tubs that David had made out of a wine barrel to use for the overnight nobles.

Cinnamon had been no help at all. She started avoiding Martine altogether, and that was just fine with her. Martine didn't like the whore and wished that David would get rid of her, but he'd told her he wouldn't. It had something to do with a deal that the whore and his father had made years ago.

"Why are you here so early?" he asked, pulling her into his arms and giving her a hug. They'd been kissing when they weren't being watched, but privacy was scarce here, and Martine longed for more time alone with David.

"I wanted to surprise you, but you seem to be up and dressed so I guess you couldn't sleep either."

"I was dreaming about you," he said, sounding sexy.

"What about me?" she asked.

"Let's just say it was a very improper dream to have."

"Not any more improper than the ones I've been having about you," she said with a giggle. She had been dreaming of coupling with David lately. Each day she spent at his side only made her want to make love with him even more.

"Shhh," he said. "I hear something."

"That's just the dog panting."

"The dog?" asked David, looking around his feet. "What is Patch doing in here?"

"Oh, is he your dog?" she asked. "The poor thing was shaking from the cold."

"He lives in the stables," David told her. "He's just old and that's why he shakes. Plus, he is afraid of just about everything. He's never even come inside before because he's always too frightened. How did you get him in here?" David bent down and pet the dog.

"He followed me in. I had to coax him a little with the dried beef and bread that I brought, but I think he was hungry."

"You are amazing, Martine. We've been trying for years to get old Patch inside and he'd never come. He sleeps in the stables with James."

"Where is James?" asked Martine. "Still sleeping? He usually hears when I arrive but he didn't come from the stables today to greet me. My horse is tied up outside the door."

"I let James sleep inside by the fire when it's really cold and we don't have any of our customers' horses for him to watch. See? There he is." David pointed across the room at the fire glowing on the hearth. There was a bump on the ground under a blanket and she realized it must be James. Patch wandered over and laid down with his back against the boy.

"I'd better put my horse in the stable," said Martine.

"I'll do it." David grabbed a cloak from the wall and threw it around his shoulders. "I have to get more wood for the fire anyway."

"I'm coming with you," she told him, following him out the door.

David offered to go out in the cold because he was hoping to cool down from the heated dream he'd been having about Martine. In his dream, he was bedding her in the hay of the loft above the stables and she was screaming out in passion as he brought her to climax over and over again. He took the reins of the horse and headed to the stables with Martine clinging to his arm.

"What are you thinking about?" she asked, making his heart jump. It was almost as if she were invading his thoughts.

"You don't want to know."

"Yes, I do," she said as they entered the stable to take care of her horse.

David lit a lantern and she helped him get the horse watered and settled.

"James will feed the horse as soon as he awakes. I'll make sure of it." He reached over and pet her horse on the nose. "I'd better go get more wood for the fire."

"Nay," she said, grabbing him by the arm. "Not until you tell me."

"Tell you what?"

"I want to hear about that improper dream involving me."

"Nay, you don't." He chuckled thinking how shocked she'd be if she really knew.

"I'll be the judge of that. Now, spill your secrets."

"Martine, if I tell you, you'll hate me."

"No, I won't." She pressed up against him. "Please?"

"Weeeeeell, I don't know." He ran a hand through his hair.

"I'll tell you about my dream if you tell me yours."

"I suppose that would be fair," he said with a nod. "As long as you swear you won't think less of me afterwards."

"I'll most likely only think of you more." She lifted her chin and kissed him, running her hand down his chest.

"It took place up there. In the hayloft." He lifted the lantern and pointed.

"Really. I've never been in a hayloft before. I'd like to see it."

"I don't think that would be a good idea." Too late. She was already at the ladder leading to the loft, looking upward.

"Ever since childhood, I've been a good climber. I was always able to climb trees higher than my brother, Robin." She took a hold of the rungs and started up.

"Nay, Martine. Don't go up there," he said with a groan.

"I want you to tell me the rest of your dream when we're at the top."

David followed her up the ladder, only so she wouldn't slip and end up breaking her neck. If someone told this girl not to do something, she was sure to want to do it. He liked her spark and excitement to try new things, but her curiosity was going to get her in trouble.

"All right, so this is the hayloft," he said, holding up the lantern. "Are you happy now?"

"What are all these blankets here?" She sat down atop one and got comfortable.

"James sleeps up here in the hay sometimes. It's warmer than down below."

"Sit next to me," she said, patting the blanket next to her. "Sit down and tell me your dream now."

He hung the lantern on a hook and took a seat next to her, putting his arm around her.

"This is nice," she said, leaning her head against his chest.

"Yes. Nice and private." He kissed her atop the head.

"Tell me, now," she said, looking up at him with those beautiful eyes that seemed more green than brown in the light of the lantern.

"Martine, you are beautiful and I'm sure many men have had lusty dreams about you and that I am not the first." He cupped her cheek and kissed her softly on the lips. The kiss lingered and slowly their lips parted.

"I've never heard of any man dreaming about me before now," she told him. "Tell me more."

"We were up here in the hayloft and we were... we were..."

"Making love," she finished his sentence for him.

"Yes," he said. "How did you know?"

"I was dreaming of making love with you, too."

"I'll bet your dream wasn't as hot as mine."

"We were naked, and our bodies were pressed together," she told him, making him feel embarrassed to hear her saying this aloud.

"Martine, please. It's not proper."

"Nay, it wasn't, and I loved every minute of it. I am so tired of always being told to only do the proper thing. Were we naked in your dream as well?"

"Yes. Very much so." He reached out and let his fingers trail down her neck, fumbling with the ties of her bodice.

"Are you going to lick me?" she asked, shocking him even more.

"What?" he asked, laughing.

"I heard Cinnamon telling one of her customers to lick her and that she would lick him back. What does that mean?"

"You are precious," he said, kissing her again. "And so innocent. I love that."

"I'm not as innocent as you think," she said, surprising him once again.

"What do you mean?"

"I'm not a virgin, in case you are wondering. Therefore, if we make love, you won't be taking my maidenhead."

"You're not a virgin?" He pulled back and looked at her in question.

"It was only once and a few years ago. I was curious about it and so when the son of a baron and I were alone in the larder, we did it. Actually, he did it and I just let him. It was far from special."

David was almost relieved to hear that she wasn't a virgin. If she were, he would never even consider making love with her because he wouldn't ruin her chances of marrying a rich nobleman who wanted an untouched woman.

"Is making love supposed to feel good?" she asked, so seriously that he knew she would have to experience it herself in order to know just how good it felt.

"Would you like to find out?"

"Yes."

"I mean, do you really want to know?"

"If you mean would I like to experience it with you, then the answer is yes. Now, tell me what we did in your dream."

"I don't think I can," he said, kissing her behind the ear and letting his kisses trail down her neck, getting closer and closer to her cleavage. "However, I can show you."

· · ·

Martine welcomed David's kisses and caresses, feeling excited when his mouth touched her skin. He nibbled on her ear, causing her to almost melt in his arms. When his tongue flicked out into her ear, she gripped him tightly, feeling ever so excited.

"That's new to me," she told him.

"I'll bet you'll experience many new things before we're done."

He kissed her atop her head, breathing in her scent if she wasn't mistaken.

"Did you just sniff me?" she asked with a giggle.

"I love the smell of your hair and I never want to forget it."

"I love your hair too." She reached up kissing him atop the head and then continuing to run her hands through his locks. "Your hair is soft," she told him in surprise.

"I'm glad now I bathed in that new tub and even washed my hair."

"Mayhap someday we can take a bath together."

"Talk like that is only making me hard to hold back."

"I don't want you to hold back," she told him, feeling his fingers fumbling with the ties on her bodice. Before she realized it, his hand had slipped inside her clothing, and his fingers skimmed softly over her bare breast.

"Mmm," she moaned as they continued to kiss and his thumb flicked across her nipple. Martine felt a wave of excitement rush through her.

"We did this in my dream," he whispered against her chest as his mouth replaced his hand. It felt so good that she gripped his hair and pulled him even closer, pushing herself deeper into his mouth.

"I like this dream," she whispered as he lay her back on the hay, pulling her bodice all the way down, giving attention to her twin peaks. "What else did we do?" she asked him.

"Some of the things we did I'll have to save and tell you about next time," he whispered in her ear, still kissing her and running his hand up her leg now.

"Why?" she asked. "I want to experience everything, David."

"Slow down, my lady. Lovemaking should not be rushed. And each time we do it, I want you to experience something new." His hand cupped her womanly mound and he explored with his fingers. She moaned in delight, throwing back her head, never wanting this dream to end.

"You like that?" he asked.

"Oh, yes. Yes, I do," she said through deep breathing, feeling him slip a finger inside her. When he did, she almost cried out in excitement, knowing that David was inside her now.

"Do I need to remove my clothes?" she asked, barely able to speak.

"You were fully clothed in my dream," he whispered.

"I was? Then how did we... do it?"

"Only certain parts need to be naked. The important ones." Then he did something that surprised her. He stood up and untied his breeches, letting them fall to the floor. Her eyes drank in his manly beauty, her jaw dropping open since she could see his fully erect form in the light of the lantern. He was big. And hard. Martine was a little scared but mostly excited.

"Wow," was all she could say, her eyes fixated on his fully aroused form.

He hunkered down between her knees, leaning over her and kissing her and teasing her again, yet he didn't enter her.

The feel of his hands on her bare bottom as he readied her made her squirm beneath him in delicious anticipation.

"Oh, David," she said, raising her knees and arching her back. "I feel myself coming to life."

"Good. That was my intention," he answered with a chuckle.

"Enter me," she commanded, and he didn't object. Slowly, he slid his hardened length into her, filling her and making her feel so complete. Like silk over steel he melded with her, making her feel as if this had been what she'd been waiting for her entire life. He wasn't forceful and neither did he think of himself.

"Is this all right, Martine?" he asked her. "I don't want to hurt you."

"You could never hurt me, David. This feels so right. Like we belong together and always have."

"I agree," he whispered, moving his hips and starting the thrusting motion of the act of making love.

"God's eyes you feel so tight and hot," he growled into her ear. The man was aroused and there was no stopping him now, but then again, she didn't want to stop him. Martine felt happy, excited and a little bit naughty. She liked it and never wanted this to end.

They clung to each other, their bodies entwined, the warmth between them making her forget they were out in the cold in the loft of a barn. None of that mattered. This was the best feeling of her life. She and David were making love and no one, nothing was going to stop them from sharing their passion with each other.

"More, more, more," she said as he thrust himself in and out, each time making that excitement inside her grow even stronger. Then, she felt as if she were atop a mountain and about to burst into the sky like a bird or a cloud. "Ooooooh," she squealed in enjoyment, gripping his shoulders and lifting her hips on her own.

"Yes, yes, yeeeeees," she heard him say in a low voice that sounded like a grunt in a way. Then, she found her release and was sure he had found his as well. The heated passion between them had finally been quenched. She'd made love with the only man who had ever taken her heart and now she didn't ever want to let him go.

"That was wonderful, David," she said when they were done.

"Wait until my next dream," he said with a chuckle.

"I can't wait."

"Neither can I." He pulled her to him, hugging her tightly and protectively in his strong arms.

"I think I am falling in love with you, David," she told him before she lost the nerve.

He rolled to the side, lying next to her, still breathing heavy. "I know," he answered. "I'd be lying if I said I didn't have strong feelings for you as well."

He pulled her back into his arms and she basked in the love between them. This felt so right, so good and so wonderful. Martine made up her mind at this moment that this was the man she wanted to spend the rest of her life with, and no one else. No matter what her father or Uncle

Corbett said, she didn't care. She loved David and never wanted to lose him.

"Marry me, David," she said, throwing caution to the wind.

After the wonderful intimate time they'd just spent together, she didn't expect him to say anything but yes. But when he remained silent, and then his arms slowly released her, a sad feeling enveloped her because she felt as if she'd just somehow ruined this special moment between them. Instead of saying he wanted to marry her too, he got up and replaced his breeches and then held out his hand to help her to her feet.

"I hear voices outside," he told her. All expression was gone from his face. There was no passion in his eyes anymore. "My cousin is most likely up and looking for me. It wouldn't be good to be caught in this situation."

"I suppose not," she said, getting up and putting her clothes back into place. Right now, she really didn't care who knew that they'd just made love in the hay. She wanted to shout it from the highest mountaintop because of the love swelling up inside her. But David didn't. All of a sudden, he didn't seem so sure about them anymore. "David?" she said, still wanting him to respond and say that he wanted to marry her too. "Did you hear what I said to you?"

"We'll talk later, my lady." He guided her to the ladder, grabbing the lantern along the way. "Right now, we need to get back to the tavern before anyone finds out just what we've done.

CHAPTER II

"Lady Martine, are you all right?" asked Cecelia later that day.

Martine kept her nose in the ledger and spoke only when she needed to when dealing with David. She wasn't sure if she'd scared him off telling him she loved him and wanted to marry him, but at the time she thought he felt the same way about her. She supposed this was all her fault. Martine was the kind of person who knew exactly what she wanted in life and went after it. Mayhap David was still unsure. She decided if she just gave him a little space and time then mayhap he'd come around. When she went back to the castle later tonight, she'd have to talk with Sage and Josefina. Since they were commoners at one time, mayhap this reaction from David was a normal thing. She just wasn't sure.

"Yes, Cecelia, I'm fine. Why do you ask?" Martine did her best to smile and pretend that nothing was bothering her.

The dog had followed her again, and was sticking to her like he never wanted her to leave. Too bad she couldn't say the same about David.

"Oh, no reason. It just seems like you and David are at odds today, but mayhap I'm imagining things."

Martine sat at a table at the far side of the tavern since customers had been coming in for the past few hours. She wanted to stay far away from everyone until she could sort things out.

"We are fine. There is just a lot of work to do, but things are starting to look up."

"You mean with the inn?" asked the pregnant girl excitedly, rubbing her belly.

"Yes."

"Do you think the funds will be there soon to pay off all the rent we owe?"

"Yes," said Martine. "Things are going well. I am sure the coffers will be filled soon and the debt will be able to be repaid."

"Oh, that is wonderful news," said the girl, her face glowing. "I was afraid I'd have to birth my baby in a stable and raise it in the wild."

"No, no, Cecelia." Martine laughed. "Everything is going to be fine. You don't need to worry. Excuse me, I need to put this ledger back with the cash box. Customers are starting to arrive and I don't want them to see where David keeps it."

"He's the only one with the key to the secret place," said Cecelia. "I hardly think the money is in any danger."

"You're probably right," said Martine, getting up from the table. Patch growled lowly, surprising her. "What's the matter, boy?" she asked, bending over to pet the dog with the ledger books tucked under her arm.

"Who let that flea-ridden thing in here?" Cinnamon walked up, glaring at the dog. Patch continued to growl and now Martine realized that the dog didn't like the whore. "Go! Get out of here!" Cinnamon reached down as if she were going to hit the dog, but David came up behind her and grabbed her wrist.

"Don't touch my dog," he warned the hussy.

"That dog doesn't like me. I want it gone," commanded Cinnamon.

"Mayhap the dog is a good judge of character," said Martine.

"What is that supposed to mean?" The whore glared at her.

"She didn't mean anything by it. Now go, get to work," said David, releasing her wrist.

"I'll go, but since she took away all of my rooms but one, I can't make money anymore. I'm going to go broke, David. Tell her to give me back the extra rooms for my clients."

"I can't do that," said David. "Lady Martine has been helping us, and I agree with all of her changes."

"All of them?" asked Martine, getting a strange look from David. He knew what she meant. There was one of her ideas that for some reason he did not agree with at all and that was marriage. For the life of her, she couldn't understand his quick change of mood from this morning.

"I need to get that back under lock and key with the cash box," said David, taking the ledger from her. She followed. He went behind the drink board and used his key to open a secret compartment. He slipped the ledger in with the box and closed it up and locked it once again.

"We need to talk, David," she told him.

"It's not a good time," he said, busying himself behind the drink board. "I have a feeling we're going to be busy tonight. Now that the Mountain Magic has arrived and word has gotten out, the business is picking up quickly just like you said. Please be sure to thank your cousin's great-grandfather for letting us purchase it and for giving us such a good price."

"I will," said Martine. "David, your debts will be able to be paid off in full soon if we can keep this up." She took a seat at a high stool at the drink board.

"We have you and your excellent skills to thank for that." He filled up the metal goblet and slid it across the drink board. "Sweet mead for Lady Martine."

"Thank you, David." She purposely reached out for it, touching his fingers, letting them linger. He looked up and they exchanged a look of love.

He leaned over and whispered to her. "Please, don't think I didn't cherish what happened this morning."

"You mean in the hayloft? She took a sip of the mead, swallowing it down, loving the taste.

"Yes."

"I understand. You are just the type of man who doesn't want to get married."

"I didn't say that. It's not true." He seemed so upset by her words when she was only trying to comfort him and give him time to sort out his feelings.

"Take your time," she told him, reaching out and putting her hand over his. "I'm in no hurry. I know what I want, but

I can see you are still unsure. I didn't mean to put you in this awkward position. I know you feel uncomfortable since I am a noble."

"Nay, it's not that. Not at all." He pulled his hand away from her and ran both his hands over his face, letting out a deep breath.

"What is it, David?" she asked, taking another sip of mead. "You know you can tell me anything. I don't want us to keep anything from each other. That is why I told you about," she leaned forward and whispered, "about me not being a virgin."

"I know," he said, still seeming flustered about something. "I respect that, Martine. And I respect you in every aspect."

"Why, thank you," she said, continuing to enjoy her mead. The tavern would start filling up with customers soon and she would need to go supervise the kitchen while the men drank. She didn't mind being in the tavern, but it seemed to make David uncomfortable since she was a noblewoman. She did her best to stay out of sight as much as possible. "I've helped Farley and your mother plan some food dishes that are easy to make and that don't cost a lot of money. Some of them will be made in smaller portions and only when the nobles occupy the tavern. We are going to try a new pottage dish out tonight."

"Martine, I cannot thank you enough for all you've done for us." He put his hand over hers, looking into her eyes like he wanted to kiss her. He wouldn't. Not with people arriving, and he was right. It wouldn't be proper.

"David?" came a female voice from behind her.

Startled, Martine quickly pulled away from David, and turned to look at the door.

"Ava!" David stood up straight and pulled down his tunic to cover his waist. "Come in," he told the girl, hurrying over to her side. There was a man behind who looked to be about five years older than her carrying what looked like a leather travel bag. "Oldrich," said David with a nod.

"Who is that woman at the drink board you are talking to?" asked the girl.

"Come. Let me introduce you." He walked Ava over to Martine. "Lady Martine, this is Ava Swift and her brother, Oldrich," said David.

"My lady," said the man, hitting his sister on the arm as he bowed. She finally curtsied.

"Ava, Lady Martine owns the inn now and is helping us make money," explained David.

"She owns the inn?" The girl didn't act as if she liked the sound of this. "David, what happened? This isn't at all what we'd planned."

"Excuse me?" said Martine, the curiosity getting the better of her. "But who exactly are you and how do you know David?"

"I have known him from childhood," Ava told her. "I am the daughter of a baker in Northumbria. We both used to live there before David moved here with his family. I've been waiting for him to call for me for over a year now. When he didn't, I decided I needed to come here to see him personally."

"Whatever for?" asked Martine, noticing the way David seemed to be suddenly fidgety. She picked up her goblet for another sip of mead.

"Whatever for?" repeated the girl, taking a hold of David's arm so tightly that it made Martine feel uncomfortable. She didn't want anyone holding on to him like that unless it was she. "David, didn't you tell, Lady Martine?"

"Tell me what?" asked Martine, her eyes flicking over to David and then back to the girl.

"We are betrothed," Ava announced. "David and I are going to get married."

CHAPTER 12

"Married?" Martine almost choked on her mead when she heard Ava's reason for coming to the tavern. David ran over to Martine and patted her on the back to stop her from coughing. "I'm fine," she told him, not sure if she was angry with him or not. What was going on here?

"Martine," said David. "Mayhap I should have mentioned that Ava and I made a promise a long time ago when we were children to someday be married. To each other."

"Yes, to each other. I understand that part," she said through squinted eyes, knowing now why he'd turned so cold when she'd mentioned marriage in the hayloft. "I suppose that would have been a good thing to mention to me before now."

"I wanted to tell you. Honest, I did," he said under his breath.

"Did you." It wasn't a question, but more of a way for

her to tell him she was severely disappointed in him right now. Suddenly, she was starting to have second thoughts about the man. Had he purposely deceived her? Or had he changed his mind about Ava once he met her? Either way, she needed to know, but this wasn't the right time to ask.

"Our fathers made an agreement that we'd be married when I turned eighteen, and now I am eighteen." The girl smiled at David as he stood in between them now, acting as if he wasn't sure which of them to stand by. "We must get married at once, David. I can't be an old maid. We have to marry right now or why bother?"

Why bother? Martine had just turned twenty and she was still not married. What was this girl's real rush?

"That's right," said her brother, Oldrich. "My sister will be married as soon as our father arrives here next week. David, where is your father?"

"My father died a year ago," David told them.

"Your father has been dead for that long and you couldn't send me a missive to tell me?" asked the girl, sounding much too stuffy and haughty for a commoner. This kind of behavior she'd expect from a noble, but not from the daughter of a baker.

"What difference would it have made?" asked David. "He died quickly from a bad heart. There was nothing you or any of us could do."

"I thought I heard voices out here." Cecelia came from the kitchen with her sister, Matilda. "Ava Swift, is that you?"

"It is." Ava ran over to hug both of David's sisters.

. . .

David felt like hiding under a rock and dying right now. He was down on his luck lately but this was something he hadn't expected to happen. When he'd moved here from up north, he thought he'd never see Ava again. Actually, he'd moved just to get away from her and her demanding ways. True, they'd been friends for a long time, but David never wanted to marry her. He'd only told her he would so she'd stop pestering him. He also hated the silly agreement that her father made with his father. It was a betrothal that had never included his opinion. It was done in spoken words only and nothing had ever been written down. David never intended on keeping his end of the deal, mainly because he'd never wanted to marry the girl to begin with. He also thought since his father was dead, the agreement no longer held up.

"David, is the tavern open already?" His mother came out of the kitchen drying her hands on a cloth. Joe and Dirk were right behind her.

"Hello, Mrs. Stone," said Ava.

His mother's mouth fell open. "Ava Swift? Oldrich? What are you two doing here? It's been so long since we've seen you."

"She's come to marry David," Martine spoke up, pushing away her empty goblet. "To keep the agreement David's father and her father made years ago betrothing them."

"Oh, well, that was a long time ago." His mother nervously looked over at David. "Elrod has passed away, so I'm sure that agreement is no longer binding."

"Our fathers shook on it," said Oldrich. "Or does that mean nothing to you?"

"Of course it means something." Cinnamon had been

spying on them again and came strutting down the stairs. "It means Lady Martine won't get David for herself after all."

"What?" shouted Ava. "David, is there something going on between you and this noblewoman?"

Before he could answer, Martine spoke up. "Mayhap you should ask him if there's something going on between him and the whore instead." It shocked David to hear Martine talk this way. Why would she even say it? She got to her feet and walked over to Ava. "Excuse me, but the tavern is not open yet so you and your brother will have to leave."

"Leave?" Ava's gaze shot over to David. "David, tell her I'm staying. I'm not going anywhere until Father shows up and this marriage takes place."

"We've just traveled for days to get here," said her brother. "Since this is an inn, we will take a room."

"I have a room for you, handsome," said Cinnamon, focusing in on Oldrich.

"Enough!" shouted Martine. "Now, I'm sorry but the rooms are not yet ready for guests. You'll have to come back later."

"Actually, we just cleaned the rooms," said Matilda. "They are ready."

"Then I'll stay here. Oldrich, are you coming?" Ava pushed past the others. Her brother followed her up the stairs.

"I'll show you to your room," said Cinnamon, disappearing up the stairs and down the hall with them.

David looked over at Martine and he almost thought she was about to cry.

"Excuse me," she said, hurrying through the kitchen. He

heard the door of the family's living quarters slam closed and knew that is where she went.

"Boy, you've gotten yourself into a lot of trouble," said Uncle Joe from behind his mother.

"He's got three women and I have none?" Dirk shook his head and left through the kitchen.

"You upset Ava," said Matilda.

"Mayhap we should go and comfort her," suggested Cecelia. The two girls hurried to the upper rooms.

David made his way behind the drink board and grabbed the bottle of whisky. He sat down at the table running his hand through his hair.

"What are you going to do?" asked his mother, slowly sitting down on the bench next to him.

"I don't know," said David. "I've never had such problems in my life. I also never wanted to marry Ava, but no one ever asked me how I felt."

"All I'm going to say is that your father would never make you honor that deal with the baker's daughter if he had known you didn't want to marry Ava," continued Greta.

"I agree," said Uncle Joe. "Especially now. If he were alive and knew you'd have a chance to marry a noblewoman instead, he'd break that other agreement in a second." Uncle Joe turned and left the room.

"David?" asked his mother, reaching out and holding his hand. "Do you perhaps have feelings for Lady Martine? It seems that Dirk and Joe think you do."

"I don't know anything anymore," he said, pulling his hand away from his mother and taking another drink. "I thought I did, but now I'm confused. I mean, I was good friends with Ava my whole life, but I don't want to marry her. On the other hand, I barely know Lady Martine, yet I can't picture going through life without her."

"Then tell them both that."

"How can I? I mean, Father made the agreement when I was just a child. He was good friends with Ava's father and they shook on it. You know how neither of them ever broke their word. That's what made their friendship so strong. Father would turn over in his grave if he knew I wanted to break his promise."

"David, I realize you were close to your father, and also that you have always wanted to do the right thing to please him, but he's gone now. Whatever deals he made no longer matter. This is your life. You can do what you want with it. Never forget that."

Before David could tell her that he wanted to send Ava away because he had feelings for Martine, the door to the kitchen opened and Dirk walked out with Martine.

"I'll be back," said Dirk. "I'm taking Lady Martine back to the castle."

"What?" David's head snapped up. "Why? It's still early."

"You'll have all the money you need to save your inn in the next day or two, I'm sure of it," Martine told him. "You don't need me to help you anymore so there is no need for me to stay." Martine collected her cloak from the table. Dirk hurried to help her don it.

"Please, don't leave now. Not like this," said David. "I don't want it to end this way between us."

"I think I've made a mistake, David. I'll be going back to the castle now where I belong."

"Martine, I mean, Lady Martine, you can't leave," said David. "What will I do without you?"

"You're a clever man," she told him. "I'm sure you can figure out how to get the rest of the money on your own." She thought he was talking about the inn, but he was really talking about their future.

"David, is there a dowry that comes with marrying Ava?" Dirk asked right in front of Martine. He could be so insensitive sometimes. "Mayhap her father could pay off the rest of our debt so we can get the deed back from Lady Martine."

"No, there is no need for that," said Martine softly. "I won't make you all leave, because I am not a mean person. Just notify me when you hold all the funds and I will return with the deed to your inn."

"Please, stay." David got up, still holding the bottle of whisky. "I need you."

She looked down at the bottle and then back up at him. "Mayhap you have your needs and wants confused, David. When you figure out which is which, let me know. Until then, I won't be back."

Dirk escorted Lady Martine out the door and to the stable to get her horse. David sank down atop the bench, feeling like his life was over.

"What are you going to do?" asked his mother.

"About the inn?"

"Nay. About your broken heart."

"She's a noble, Mother. I'm only fooling myself to think we could end up together. She deserves someone so much better than me."

"And what about you, David?" she asked. "Don't you

deserve some happiness in life as well?"

"I am naught but a commoner. I belong with someone who is more like—"

"Like Ava?" His mother didn't wait for an answer. She got up and left the room, leaving David alone with his thoughts. He took another swig of whisky and laid his pounding head on the table.

"What the hell is the matter with you, boy?" came his uncle's voice from the darkness. With the tapping noise of his cane, he made his way to the table and sat down. "Fight for what you want. You're a Stone. Stones are solid like a rock. Nothing shakes us."

"Well, this sure has me shaken," mumbled David.

"If you love her, then go after her, boy! Don't let the best thing in your life walk right out that door."

"How can I?" He felt as if every bit of hope was gone. "She doesn't want me. Not anymore. She thinks I'm nothing but a scoundrel and she is probably right."

"What the hell does that mean?"

"Uncle Joe, I was betrothed and yet that didn't stop me from kissing Lady Martine. I could have told her I was destined to marry Ava, but I didn't. I could have told her I've lain with Cinnamon more times than I can count, but instead I made it seem like I never had."

"Don't think she's a fool. She knows about you and the whore and now she knows about you marrying Ava as well. What did you expect her to do? Stay here when you have both of them? What do you need her for? Of course she had to leave. She's a lady. No lady worth her salt would stay and watch you make an ass of yourself." Joe grunted and stood, shaking his head. "If I wasn't afraid of missing and hitting the goddamned bench, I'd kick you in the ass right now, David. You are nothing like your father. He never would have let anyone or anything stand in his way once he made up his mind that he wanted something. You disgrace the family name."

David got up and slowly walked back to the drink board still clinging to the bottle of whisky. He put it down right next to Lady Martine's silver goblet that held the remains of her sweet mead.

Martine was sweet just like that honeyed drink. She was sweet and smart and wonderful in every way. She made him feel alive when he'd felt dead for years now. What the hell was he so afraid of? She'd admitted to having feelings for him, so mayhap she still did. Or didn't. Either way, his uncle was right. He couldn't just let her walk out his door and out of his life forever. He had to fight for what– for who he wanted.

He put down the bottle and got his cloak from his living quarters, stopping in the kitchen to give his mother a quick kiss.

"What is that for?" she asked.

"For luck," he told her.

"Why do I need luck?" she asked him, cutting up vegetables to make pottage for tonight's guests.

"Not luck for you, but for me, Mother. I'm going after what I want and I hope I won't be disappointed with the results." He turned and left the kitchen.

"Wait, David. Where are you going?" his mother called after him.

"Open the tavern as usual and tell Dirk to tend to the drink board tonight. I'm not sure when or if I'll be back."

CHAPTER 13

"Thank you for the escort, Dirk, but you don't need to go any farther." Martine stopped her horse at the entrance to Blake Castle, embarrassed by returning so soon when she'd told her guard not to get her before midnight.

"Will you be coming back to the inn tomorrow?" Dirk wanted to know.

"Nay, I'm sorry. I don't think so."

"If it's because of Ava, don't let that bother you," said Dirk. "I don't really think David wants to marry her. Besides, once Ava finds out my cousin has enjoyed the pleasures of the tavern's whore on more than one occasion, she'll most likely want nothing to do with him anyway. She's rather haughty for the daughter of a baker."

Martine's heart ached just a little more when Dirk had to mention Cinnamon. She was pretty sure that David had known the pleasures of the whore but still she wasn't certain. It made it easier to handle that way. Hearing it now confirmed by Dirk only made things even worse than what she thought they were.

"Tell your aunt I'm sorry to leave this way, but I had to go."

"Are you saying you won't help us anymore?"

"I wish I could, but I just can't. Not with things being what they are."

"What's going to happen when Lord Corbett returns?" asked Dirk. "Will he kick us out and take away our business?"

"I'm afraid the answer is yes unless you have all the money owed to him. I don't think he will be as forgiving as I was."

"Forgiving? Excuse me, my lady, but I don't think you're being very forgiving at all. At least not where David is concerned."

"What?" Her head snapped up.

"I'm sorry, I said too much. If you'll excuse me, my lady, I really need to get back and help at the tavern."

"Of course. Thank you, Dirk."

Dirk grunted and took off on his horse down the road. Martine rode into the courtyard in deep thought. Why did she feel as if she was the one who had done something wrong? She was only trying to help David and his family. David was the one who had deceived her and she didn't like that at all. She couldn't go back to the inn again. It was over.

After stabling her horse, Martine made her way to the great hall, hearing a lot of happy commotion coming from within. The minstrels were playing music and there was a feast in progress even though it wasn't time yet for the meal.

"What's going on in there?" asked Martine, stopping a servant in the corridor to ask him.

"Didn't you hear?" asked the boy. "Lord Corbett has returned."

"What?" she gasped in surprise. "Already?" She had hoped David and his family would have at least a few more days to raise the rest of the rent money. Now, she almost wished she had stayed at the inn to help them, after all.

"Yes," said the boy. "Lord Robin and Lord Madoc returned with him as well. They've all just seen baby Martin and Lord Corbett ordered a celebration feast."

"My father is here too?" That horrified Martine more than the fact that her uncle was back.

"Yes, my lady. Here he comes now," said the boy, bowing and running back to the kitchen.

"Martine, I've been looking for you." Her father, Madoc, walked over with a tankard in his hand. "Someone told me you were at the Cross Hare Inn. What a coincidence. That is where we are meeting up with Lords Rook, Gar, and Garrett later on tonight. We won the skirmish for our king and we're going there to celebrate."

"Eleanor's father is going to be there too? But he's Lord Warden of the Cinque Ports."

"Yes, of course, he is. He'll be there as well."

"Why don't you celebrate right here? In the castle?" she asked, feeling nervous and a bit panicked. She knew David's tavern was not in shape to host so many important noblemen. Not yet. She still had things planned to do to make it ready. Plus, Martine wasn't in a hurry to remind her uncle that David was so far behind with his rent.

"We were going to stay here at the castle, but Lord Rook

suggested the Cross Hare Inn instead. He said we would find it intriguing for some reason."

"Yes, I'm sure he did. Excuse me, Father. I see my cousin now and I'd like to thank him for making that suggestion." Martine beelined it across the great hall, grabbing Rook but the arm and yanking him away from the other knights.

"God's eyes, Martine, what's the matter with you?" snapped Rook, looking down to his tunic. "You made me spill ale on my tunic."

"The spilled ale is the least of your worries because I am about to wring your neck."

Rook laughed. "What has come over you? You're acting odd. What are you even doing here? Rose told me that Josefina told her that you now help out the Stone family at the Cross Hare Inn. Is this true?"

"It is."

"I also heard that you've got eyes for the proprietor. Donald, was it?"

"Nay, that's not his name, and it's none of your business if I have eyes for him or not. Rook, how could you invite Uncle Corbett, my father, and even the Lord Warden to the inn tonight? What is the matter with you?"

Rook chuckled. "I just thought this way we'd all get a look at the man you've fallen for."

"Please tell me you didn't say anything about David to my father or Uncle Corbett."

"David, that's his name! That's right. Nay, I didn't tell them about you kissing him, if that's what you're worried about."

Martine closed her eyes, hoping to hell he didn't know what else she'd done with David. "You know about the kissing?" She could have died on the spot. "Is no secret safe with Josefina and Sage?"

Rook took a swig of ale and playfulness danced in his bright blue eyes. "They didn't tell me about the kissing, I just took a gamble and it paid off. You've given yourself away, Martine." He chuckled lowly, seeming to really enjoy this.

"Rook, you must change their minds about meeting at the tavern tonight. Please. I beg you."

"Take it easy, Martine. My father doesn't change plans once they're made. I won't mention anything about you kissing David, I promise. However, I do want to get a good look at the man for myself."

"You don't know what you've done. You're going to endanger David and his entire family."

"How so?" Rook looked over the rim of his tankard taking another drink of ale.

"Didn't Raven tell you what happened?"

"I think she said she got ill and had to return to the castle. Why?"

"Not that! I am talking about the fact that the Cross Hare Inn is four months late in paying their rent."

"Ooooooh," he said and shrugged. "Well, then Father will be taking the inn back from David tonight I guess. Too bad for him."

"Nay, he won't be taking the inn back from David," said Martine.

"Why not?" asked Rook.

"Oh, never mind!" she said in frustration, hurrying up the stairs to her chamber. She had to do something to help David. She couldn't let him suffer the way he was about to, even if she hated him right now for lying to her and keeping things from her. She had to warn David so many nobles were coming. They had to prepare.

She paced back and forth in her room, not knowing what to do. She didn't want to see David and his family thrown out on the street and their business taken away from them. But with so many important noblemen meeting there tonight, it was evident that Lord Corbett would remember about the late rent. They were so close to having the money to pay off the entire debt. Why couldn't the men have waited a few more days before coming home?

There was a knock on the door, irritating Martine even more. "Whoever it is, go away," she shouted. When the knocking continued, she rushed over and pulled open the door. A man covered in a long cloak and wearing a hood over his head stood there with his face downward.

"Who are you and what do you want?" she snapped.

"Lady Martine, it's me." The man raised his face and she saw that it was David.

Just when David expected Martine to slam the door in his face, she surprised him by gripping the front of his tunic and pulling him into the room with her. She looked both ways up and down the corridor and then slammed the door and locked it.

"All right," he said, scratching the side of his face. "Does this mean you hate me or love me again? I'm confused. I've never been in a position like this before."

"How did you sneak into the castle and up to my

chamber without a guard even stopping you?" she asked him.

"There was a lot of commotion going on downstairs so it wasn't hard to walk right in."

"That is all the fuss over my new nephew," she told him.

"Oh, baby Martin," said David with a smile. "How is the little fellow doing? I'd love to stop in and see him for myself." He looked back at the door.

"Forget about the baby, you have bigger problems on your hands right now."

"Oh, yes, I know. I've been a fool and I want to apologize to you."

"What?" she asked, acting as if she couldn't believe he was saying this right now, when it seemed like a big issue back at the tavern.

He cleared his throat and tried again. "Martine, I am heartily sorry that I didn't tell you I laid with the whore or that I am betrothed to be married. I know that was wrong. Honestly, once I met you none of that even mattered anymore, so I didn't think it was a good idea to bring it up." He lowered his hood and waited.

"Doesn't matter?" Her face was stone-like, and he couldn't read her mood.

"Well, yes, it matters, of course, it does," he said, trying to say what he thought she wanted to hear. "I mean, mayhap it matters. I'm not really sure. I just meant that I– Martine I am smitten with you."

"Smitten," she repeated, making him very nervous. Mayhap that wasn't the best choice of words. After all, they had made love today.

"Do you have to keep repeating what I say?" he asked,

pacing back and forth. "I am not good with words and this is hard for me. I want you to know that I am trying to go after what I want, even though what I want is you and it's terrifying because you're a noble and I'm a commoner and I don't know what you want me to say." He ran it all together, hoping some of this made some sense as to how he felt.

"What I want you to say," she repeated his words once more.

"Martine, put it this way." He took a deep breath and looked up at the ceiling, holding up one finger. Then he nodded, believing he finally found the right words to say. "I think I'm falling in love with you."

That shut her up. She backed up and slowly lowered herself atop the bed, holding on to the carved wooden spindle.

"Think?" Once again, she repeated his word.

"Know. I know I am," he quickly corrected himself, hoping he hadn't already ruined his only chance to get her back. Once again, he looked up at the ceiling, this time noticing the iron posts and bedcurtains hanging around the humongous bed. "Wow, I just noticed how elegant this room is. The whole castle is bigger and more elaborate than I'd ever dreamed. I've never been in here before, you realize. It was only by luck that I heard Lord Rook mention you went to your chamber. I climbed the stairs and thought I saw someone going into this room and hoped to hell it was you."

"You are lucky not to have knocked on another noble's door, like my uncle's," she told him.

"I take risks. It's what I do," he told her, not sure she'd believe it, but after all he'd taken a huge risk in coming here.

"Martine? Are you in there?" A knocking at her door panicked David.

"My father," whispered Martine, springing up off the bed. "She grabbed David and shoved him into an adjoining room that was filled with clothes. "Stay in the wardrobe and don't make a sound," she whispered. "If he finds you here you'll be thrown in the dungeon and most likely condemned to death."

"Great," he mumbled into the hanging clothes. Well, this is what he got for going after what he wanted. He took a risk and now he was about to be sentenced to death for it. Well, at least if he was imprisoned and sentenced to die, it would be for a good cause. Now he wouldn't die before having told Lady Martine that he loved her.

"Martine?" The door opened and her father's head peeked around into the room. "Why didn't you answer me?"

"Father," said Martine, feeling her heart drumming so loudly in her ears that she wondered if her father could hear it too. No matter what happened, she had to keep David hidden.

"Can I come in?" he asked.

"I was just going down to the great hall to see the baby again. We'll go together," she told him, meaning to leave the room.

"No need for that." He opened the door wider and she could see a big group of people standing behind him.

"What's this?" she asked, seeing all the eyes watching her.

"Hello, Martine," said Rose, Rook's wife, pushing her

way to the front of the crowd. "Your father told us you seemed a little down and we came up here to cheer you up."

"How thoughtful of you all." Martine couldn't stop thinking of what would happen once they all found David hiding in her wardrobe. It wasn't going to be good.

"I thought seeing Martin would cheer you up." Sage walked into the room carrying the baby. Josefina was right behind her.

"I hope you don't mind that I invited our husbands up here too," said Josefina.

"Mind? Now why would I?" Martine really wanted to die right now. She also felt so sorry for what was about to happen to David. He came here to tell her he loved her, and this is how he'd be rewarded? Mayhap it would have been better if he'd stayed at the tavern and never tried to tell her at all.

"Oh, it looks like Gar is bringing your Uncle Corbett and Lady Devon along too," said Josefina, stretching her neck to see down the hallway.

"I also told Raven to meet us here," said Sage. "Jonathon is working at the forge and she is still feeling a little ill. It's best if she moves around."

They all walked into the room, making themselves at home. Her father carried his tankard of ale. When Gar entered the room with Rook and Robin, he had a flagon of wine and they each held a goblet. By the looks of it, they weren't planning on leaving anytime soon.

"Did you want to hold the baby?" asked Sage, pushing the baby into her arms before she had a chance to answer. "That always cheers me up." Martine sincerely doubted that her troubles could be solved right now by holding a baby.

"What is going on in here?" asked Devon as she and Raven entered the room just after Lord Corbett.

"It's good to be home," said Corbett, greeting everyone again even though he'd already most likely done so downstairs in the great hall.

"Aye, I'm happier than any of you." Lord Robin came over to collect his new baby from her. Martine gladly gave it to him, because right now she didn't want to hold a baby. All she wanted to do was to think of a way to get all these people to leave her room before David was discovered.

"So, when will Uncle Garrett be here?" asked Martine, wondering how much time she had to help David get the tavern in order before all hell broke loose. As if it hadn't already.

"The Lord Warden will be arriving with his family in a few hours," said Corbett.

"Is Eleanor coming too?" asked Martine, knowing her red-headed cousin would understand her troubles and would probably go out of her way to help her.

"I believe so," said Devon, walking over and laying her hand on Martine's shoulder. "Martine," she whispered. "Why do you look so shaken?"

"Aunt Devon, I have big problems," she whispered. Martine looked over to the wardrobe and caught David peeking out. When he saw her looking, he disappeared within again.

Devon gasped, having seen him as well.

"It's not what you think," whispered Martine. "Well, not really. Please help me, Aunt Devon. I'm going to be in such big trouble." Thankfully, the woman had a heart.

"I think it is much too stuffy up here with all these

people," announced Devon. "It's not good for the baby. Let's go down to our solar, Corbett. It's much larger and more comfortable there."

"Oh, good idea, dear. This way everyone can sit." Corbett led the way with his tankard held high in the air.

"Good luck, my dear. It's all up to you now," whispered Devon, giving Martine a quick hug and being the last one to exit the room and close the door.

"David, you can come out now," said Martine, spinning around to see Rook standing in the corner in the shadows with his arms crossed over his chest.

She cringed as David walked out of the wardrobe, brushing himself off. "There are moths in there, Martine, did you know that?"

"We've got bigger problems than moths right now." Her eyes fixated on Rook. David turned to see him and his jaw dropped.

"Lord Rook, it's not what you're thinking. I swear." He held out a hand, as if that would keep Rook from him.

"And what would I be thinking?" Rook walked forward slowly like a predator going after its prey. "Just because there is a man hiding in the wardrobe and my cousin is acting very guilty, why should I think anything bad at all?"

"Stop, it Rook!" Martine burst forward and pounded on Rook's chest. "I hate you. You are trying to ruin my life. Stop it, I say!"

"Whoa, now," said Rook, grabbing Martine by the wrists. "I knew downstairs you were hiding something but I had no idea what you were hiding was a man in your wardrobe."

"I'm David Stone. From the Cross Hare Inn," said David

with a slight bow, as if right now that would make any difference.

"I figured," said Rook strolling over to the window and looking out. "I also figure you are here because you came to profess your undying love for my cousin, Martine."

"Well, yes. Sort of," said David. "I mean, I'm not sure it's gotten to the level of undying yet, but I do love her."

Rook's head jerked around. "Let's hope that love hasn't gone too far. Because I would hate to be the one to tell her father about it."

Martine and David looked at each other but neither of them said a word. Martine realized she had to say something and fast.

"Rook, David and I are in love and we want to get married."

"Yes. I want to marry her," said David.

"I don't like this." Rook looked at them suspiciously, probably figuring out that they'd already made love.

"I don't care whether or not you like it because–" Martine stopped when she realized just what David said. "Did you say you want to marry me?" she asked David.

"I did," he said with conviction. This surprised her since she really wasn't sure that he wasn't still planning on marrying Ava.

"What about Ava?" she had to ask.

"Who's Ava?" Rook wanted to know.

"I don't love her and I already told her I'm not marrying her."

"You did?" Martine's heart swelled.

"Who's Ava?" Rook asked again, but they both ignored him.

"And Cinnamon? What about her?" asked Martine, having to know he wouldn't look to her pleasures again.

"Cinnamon? The tavern whore?" asked Rook, knowing who she was.

"Hush, Rook, or I'll be sure to tell Rose you bedded that whore on several occasions before you met her."

"Cinnamon told you? That hussy. I thought she said she kept her clients' names a secret."

A large smile spread across Martine's face. "She didn't tell me, but you just did."

"You tricked me," spat Rook.

"I took a gamble and it paid off, that's all."

"Lord Rook, may I speak freely?" asked David with a bow.

"Of course." Rook shrugged and started to pull off his leather gloves finger by finger. Martine could see he was upset that she knew about his past trysts with the whore.

"I realize I am just a commoner and that I have no right to fall in love with Lady Martine, but it happened and that's all there is to it."

"It happened, did it?" Rook looked over at Martine.

"It did," she told him smugly.

"I made some mistakes and I'm sorry now that I wasn't totally open and honest with Martine, but I never felt as if I had a chance with her so I just wanted to cherish the moments I did have, I guess."

"Go on," said Rook.

Martine said nothing. The butterflies in her belly were flipflopping out of control.

"I plan on asking her father for her hand as soon as I can

get back on my feet and am able to pay the four months of rent that I owe."

"Four months is a lot," said Rook. "How do you plan on doing that?"

"Lady Martine holds the deed. She's been helping us lately and her ideas have paid off. I'm just a little short of having all the money I need to pay my entire debt."

"Well, I suppose having all the nobles at your tavern tonight will take care of the outstanding part."

"Nobles are coming to the Cross Hare? Tonight?" David's attention shot over to Martine.

"I was going to tell you but we had some uninvited guests and distractions," said Martine.

"Will Lord Corbett be there?"

"Yes, my father will," said Rook.

"Then it's too late. He's sure to ask me about the debt as soon as he walks in. I'm afraid there is no hope of keeping my inn now," said David. "I've run out of time. It's over."

"Oh, no it isn't," said Martine. "Remember, I told you I'd help you and your family."

"Still?" asked David. "When you left today I thought you really didn't ever want to see me again."

"We'll talk about us later," said Martine. "Right now, we need to get back to your tavern and prepare for the nobles."

"Is there anything I can do to help?" asked Rook, sounding as if he felt bad for the hornet's nest he'd poked.

"Not unless you have four months' rent," said David.

"Rook, we need time. If we can just get through tonight, I promise David will have the money he owes. I am going to give him back the deed to the inn but he needs to make a little more money yet. Can you help us?"

"I wish I could, Martine, but I'm not sure how."

"Try to persuade your father to go somewhere else tonight."

"Actually, it could work in your favor if they go to the Cross Hare Inn," Rook told her.

"How so?" asked David.

"Get to know them, David," Rook suggested. "Let them see you are a good man. And let them see you are a good proprietor as well. That way, when the time comes to ask for Martine's hand in marriage, it'll be harder for her father–and the rest of them to say no."

"Yes," agreed Martine. "Do it, David."

"I will," said David, sounding more confident than Martine ever remembered. "I will do it because nothing can stop a Stone from going after what they want. And I, Lady Martine, want you as my wife."

CHAPTER 14

Martine didn't speak much to David on the way to the inn. She wanted time to think things over. Right now, she wasn't sure how she felt about anything. She was nervous for herself but also for David. Martine would talk to David later about their relationship and if it could possibly really lead to marriage. But right now she wanted to help his family and keep them from losing their home.

They'd been so kind to Martine and her family. If it wasn't for Greta, little baby Martin might not have been born alive. This family risked everything to help her, and she wasn't going to abandon them now. Not when the nobles were about to show up at David's tavern.

"Martine, let me assist you." David was off his horse and holding out his arms to help Martine dismount. She'd been so deep in thought that she hadn't even noticed they were already at the inn.

"I'm fine," she said, starting to dismount. He helped her anyway, putting his hands around her waist and slowly lowering her down the length of his body. Her body brushed up against his and she put her hands on his shoulders to steady herself.

"There. Isn't that better?" His hands were still on her waist and he stared into her eyes. For a split second she thought he was going to try to kiss her again. For another second, she'd almost considered letting him do it. It was too risky right now. They needed to be careful. Word of them getting back to her father before she had a chance to tell him about David was only going to ruin anything between them.

"David, I'm worried for you and your family," said Martine. "I just wish we had a little more time to raise the rest of the money before you have to confront my uncle."

"Mayhap Lord Corbett won't mention the late rent tonight. There is a chance he'll be too busy celebrating with the other men to even give it a thought."

"Not likely. My uncle doesn't forget a thing."

"Then we'd better hurry. There is much to be done before your father and uncle and all the nobles arrive." He let go of her and grabbed her travel bag off her horse. Then he put his fingers in his mouth and whistled loudly.

"What was that for?" she asked, getting her answer when she saw the stable boy, James running to them from behind the inn. Following him was Patch.

"Patch! I missed you," said Martine, bending over to pet the brown dog with the white patch on his face.

"James, take our horses to the stable and water them and rub them down," instructed David.

"I will," came the boy's answer, scooping up the reins from both horses.

"There will be quite a few nobles arriving here tonight

so get one of your friends to help you in the stables," David continued. "I can't pay them right now, but I'll feed them. I'll also need them to spend the night in the stable since I'm not sure how long the nobles will be here."

"I'll find someone, don't worry," said James, heading with the horses to the stables.

"Come on, Patch," said Martine as they headed to the inn.

"Nay, the dog stays outside tonight. I have enough troubles," said David.

Martine looked down to Patch and swore he understood David since the dog looked sad. She didn't want to send the dog away.

"Surely, there's no harm in having the hound inside the tavern," she told him.

"He'll only cause trouble." David continued walking.

"I heard your cousin say there was a mouse in the tavern the other day. Mayhap, Patch will be able to catch it."

"Hah!" said David with a chuckle. "Martine, the hound is old and slow. He's too slow to catch cold."

"I don't believe that. I think if we gave Patch a chance, he'd prove his worth."

"If it'll make you happy, bring the dog inside," said David, opening the door to the tavern. "Just keep him in the kitchen tonight, away from the nobles. Also, far away from Farley and his sharp cleaver."

"You poor thing." Martine hunkered down and hugged the dog, kissing him on the head. She loved animals and felt sorry for this one. Patch licked her cheek and she giggled. "He's giving me kisses," she said, thinking the dog was just like its owner.

"That's odd. He never does that to anyone." David shrugged. "Please, my lady. I'd like to get inside and get to work."

"Of course," she said, walking with him to the tavern. Patch followed close behind.

"Lady Martine. I didn't think we'd ever see you here again." Dirk saw them from across the room and hurried over to greet them.

Patch let out a bark, sounding to Martine as if he was happy.

"Whoa!" said Dirk, jumping backward. "Did Patch just bark? He never barks at anything."

"He's happy," said Martine. "Patch just needed a little love, that's all."

There came the sound of a slamming door from upstairs and Ava appeared, looking down at them. "David? What is she doing here?" The girl slowly walked down the stairs. "And where is Oldrich? I haven't seen him all day."

"Ava, Lady Martine and I have a lot of work to do so please don't bother us," said David. "And I am not the keeper of your brother."

Another door opened upstairs and Oldrich came out of Cinnamon's room, hopping on one foot as he pulled on his boot. Cinnamon leaned on the doorway with a smug look on her face, half undressed as always.

"Oldrich, what were you doing with that hussy?" asked Ava.

"If you have to ask, sweetheart, you'll never know," cooed Cinnamon.

"David, do something about this." Ava held out her arm pointing to her brother.

"I hope you paid her," David told Oldrich.

"Of course, he did. I don't work for free." Cinnamon held up a coin and grinned.

"Don't forget to give half the money to the inn," said Martine, tired of all these distractions. "Now, if the three of you are going to keep showing up, then David and I will find jobs for you. After all, the tavern will be crowded tonight with many nobles."

"Jobs?" asked Ava, sounding shocked.

"Nobles? How many?" Cinnamon perked up, probably already counting in her head how much money she'd be making off them.

"These nobles aren't interested in what you have to offer," said Martine. "It's my father and uncle and several of my brothers-by-marriage. All married and devoted to their wives."

"Oh." Cinnamon scrunched up her nose and disappeared into the room, closing the door behind her.

"We'd be happy to help you out, David," said Oldrich. "I can pour drinks and my sister will wait tables."

"I will not," spat Ava. "David just broke our betrothal so why should I do anything for him?"

"David? Why is she still here?" asked Martine softly. "I thought you told me she was leaving."

"She is, but not until morning," David explained. "It's too dangerous for Ava and her brother to leave at nightfall."

"If you're taking up a room, then I hope you are paying for it," Martine boldly told the girl.

"Martine, I couldn't charge her," said David softly. "Not after what I did to her."

"That's right," said Ava. "After what he did by breaking our fathers' agreement, he should be paying me."

"You wouldn't." Martine looked at David and he shook his head. "Fine. Then be sure to help out tonight, because we'll need all the extra hands we can get." She didn't wait for the girl's answer. Martine headed to the kitchen with the dog following at her feet. David entered the room right behind her.

"Martine, wait," he said, putting his hand on her arm.

"You need to use my title when we're around others, David," she reminded him. "Lady Martine, is what you need to call me." She was being a little harsh with him, but she couldn't take the chance he'd forget to use her title tonight around the nobles if she should be spotted. That would not bear well for him at all.

"Of course," he said, letting his fingers slip off her arm. "Lady Martine, I'm sorry about the whole thing with Ava. You didn't deserve to have to go through that."

"What's done is done. Right now we need to focus on our goal. The first order of business is to make sure the tavern has enough food– good food to feed the nobles. And they're not going to be sharing a bowl of pottage for the table, so make certain you have enough bowls and cups for each of them."

"I'll make certain of that," said Farley from the fire, having overheard them.

"Thank you, Farley," said Martine. She noticed Patch wagging his tail and heading over to Farley.

"What's that hound doing in my kitchen?" spat Farley.

"Patch is just in here while the nobles visit," Martine told the cook. "Please, be nice to the dog."

"Hmmph," sniffed Farley, turning his back on the dog and continuing to cook.

"David? What's going on?" Greta rushed into the kitchen with her daughters right behind her.

"Lady Martine, we didn't expect to see you again," said Matilda. "Not since Ava is still here."

"Matilda, hush," said David. "We have Mar— I mean, Lady Martine's family is coming here tonight to celebrate, and we must prepare for them. Keeping the inn might all depend on how this visit goes."

Martine noticed he was about to call her Martine without her title but quickly corrected himself.

"Oh, good," said Cecelia. "That will bring in good money for the tavern."

"Not really," said David. "You know that nobles eat and drink for free. Especially Lord Corbett since he owns the land we're on. There is no way we can charge them."

"If you do a good job and the nobles are happy, I am sure they will leave money in appreciation. They are not heartless," Martine explained. "They realize you need to make a living. Besides, if they don't leave coin, I'll walk out there and suggest that they do. Don't worry."

"I'm nervous," said Cecelia. "Being pregnant, my balance is off lately and I'm afraid I might drop a tray of food on them."

"You'll be fine, dear," said Greta.

"Nay, she's right," said David. "We can't take the chance that the nobles will be disappointed. Besides, Cecelia, I told you I don't want you carrying heavy trays while pregnant. You can help in the kitchen instead."

"But we need more help at the tables," said Greta. "I

need to be back here assisting Farley with the meal so I can't do it."

"Ava will have to serve tables then," said Martine, pulling parchment and a feather pen and ink out of her bag. She sat down at the table. Patch hobbled around the kitchen sniffing everything he could.

"Ava is going to wait tables?" asked the Matilda, giggling.

"I don't think she'll like that," said Cecelia.

"If not, she'll need to assist Farley and Greta can wait tables instead," said Martine. "Didn't you say Ava is the daughter of a baker? She must know her way around a kitchen."

"Ava is lazy and couldn't boil water without instructions," said Matilda. "She never could."

"Nay. I don't want her touching the food," said David. "I'll tell her she will need to serve tables, but I'll keep her to the commoners' tables. I will serve the nobles myself if need be."

"You'll need help. They are very demanding. I will help you," said Martine, starting to make a list of things to do and who would do them."

"Nay," said David with a shake of his head. "You are a noble. You will not do such a menial job."

"No job is menial to me when it means it will benefit your family and hopefully save your home and business," said Martine.

"Nay, he's right," agreed Greta. "It would be wise to stay hidden while the nobles are here. They won't understand why you've chosen to help us," said Greta.

"Perhaps, you're right. I'll stay out of sight until I've had a chance to talk to my father about David and our plans."

David couldn't get over Martine's selflessness. He'd never met a noble in his life that would go to such extremes to help commoners. She was kind and thoughtful and so willing to do whatever needed to be done. He'd never seen anything like it before. Even Ava, the girl who he was supposed to marry, wouldn't lift a finger to help him. He knew now that he'd made the right decision to marry her over any other woman. The love in Martine's heart was admirable. He had never met anyone like her.

"Matilda, call the others in here for a quick meeting," said David. "Make certain Cinnamon and Ava come too."

A half hour later, everyone was working together to get the tavern and inn put into the best shape for the nobles' arrival this evening. Even Ava finally stopped complaining and started helping out, although it wasn't much. David figured the girl probably only did it hoping to change David's mind and say he'd marry her after all. Which he wouldn't. There was no one in the world he wanted to marry except for his angel, Martine. He prayed he could convince her father to give him her hand in marriage, because if not, he wasn't sure what he would do.

CHAPTER 15

Martine waited nervously in the kitchen of the Cross Hare Inn as her father and the rest of the nobles entered the tavern. She didn't want to be seen. If so, it would only mean trouble for David, and she didn't want that. She needed to give David time to meet and greet her father and to try to get to know him.

"It's crucial that everything goes well tonight," she told Greta, watching as the woman prepared a dish consisting of pork, root vegetables and dried currants for the nobles. Cecelia busied herself washing dishes.

"We don't have any white bread," Greta told Martine, wrapping a cloth around her hand to pull loaves of brown bread from the embers of one of the dying cookfires. "Farley said we needed more bread tonight, but they didn't have enough at the baker's so he suggested we make it this way since we don't have an oven." The bread was hot and she dropped the loaf on the table, blowing on her fingers to cool them down.

"Brown bread will be fine," said Martine. "They won't expect anything but that in a tavern."

"They're nobles and of course they'll want white bread," came a voice. Martine looked up to see Ava standing in the kitchen door.

"You?" gasped Martine, Ava being the last person she wanted to see right now. "I thought David sent you to wait on the tables of the commoners."

"I no longer feel like doing it." Ava strolled into the kitchen, acting haughty as usual. "After all, if you're going to be the wife of an innkeeper instead of me, I think you should start getting used to waiting tables."

"Ava, nay!" gasped Cecelia, looking over with a cloth in her hands.

"You cannot speak to a noblewoman in that manner," scolded Greta.

"She won't be a noblewoman once she marries David, will she?" asked Ava. "She'll be living in this small place, sharing a room with the rest of you and tending to the needs of drunkards from now on."

"How can you say that?" asked Cecelia. "Lady Martine will always be a noble, even if she marries my brother."

Martine felt a knot in her stomach. This is something she hadn't thought about at all. Her commoner sisters-by-marriage ended up with courtesy titles and living at the castle after marrying noblemen. But her situation was different. She didn't think David would feel comfortable at the castle. She was also sure he wouldn't want to give up the inn and leave his family. After all, his family needed him. He was the head of the family and his mother depended on him. His sister was going to have her baby soon, and had no husband. His cousin Dirk couldn't even read or tally a ledger, and Uncle Joe was blind. What would they all do without David? This was something Martine hadn't thought about and also something she didn't want to think about right now.

"Here, Ava. Take these loaves of bread to the noble's table." Greta hurriedly stacked the freshly baked loaves onto a tray.

"Nay. I won't do it." Ava crossed her arms over her chest and scowled at Martine. "Why would I do anything to help her? She stole my husband from me."

"David is not your husband." Martine was helping to scoop the porridge into wooden bowls, and spoke as she worked. She had even changed out of her good gown and wore one of Cecelia's gowns at the girl's insistence since she couldn't fit in it anymore. Since Martine realized kitchen work was messy, she hadn't argued, but instead donned the commoner's clothes.

"He would be my husband if it weren't for you. I won't let you get away with this." Ava stormed out of the kitchen.

"What do you think she is going to do?" asked Martine.

"Oh, don't worry about Ava. You have much more important things to tend to right now," said Greta, loading the bowls of food onto the tray. "Where is Matilda? She needs to bring this tray to the noble's table since Ava won't do it. The food is going to get cold."

"I'll see if I can motion to Matilda to come in here." Martine peeked out the door, looking for David's younger sister. The room was crowded and she didn't see the girl anywhere. David was behind the drink board while Dirk brought tankards of ale to the nobles. Joe sat at the door, holding on to his cane waiting for Oldrich to hand him the entry fees collected so he could bounce them on the board.

"Raise a cup with me to celebrate that we are home and alive," said her father lifting his cup in the air.

"Aye," answered Lord Corbett, following suit. The rest of the men laughed heartily and spoke loudly, while banging their fists against the table. David came over from the drink board with a bottle in his hand.

"I'd like to introduce myself," said David. "I am David Stone, proprietor of the Cross Hare Inn and would like to welcome you all here tonight."

"Hello, David," said Madoc, eying up the bottle in his hand. "What have you got there?"

Before he could reply, Ava walked up to the table. "I'm Ava Swift," she told the nobles getting odd looks from them. "I'm betrothed to David."

"That's nice," remarked one of the men, not caring in the least. Until they heard what she had to say next.

"David, however is in love with a noblewoman, so he says. He's scorned me for someone he can't even have but thinks that he will convince one of you to let him marry her."

"What does that mean?" asked Madoc.

"What's going on here?" growled Lord Gar.

"Oh, no!" Martine put her hand to her mouth. The foolish girl was going to ruin everything.

"Who wants Mountain Magic?" asked David, holding up the bottle and trying to distract the men. "No charge tonight for the nobles."

"David, no," Martine whispered, since the whisky would

bring in good money. That is, money that David needed to pay off his debts.

"Free Mountain Magic? How can we say no to that?" asked the Lord Warden, holding out his cup. "Fill it up, David."

The distraction worked, but not for long. As soon as they had their drinks, Cinnamon strolled over to the table, running her hand along the backs of the nobles who were all married.

"I'm available for any or all of you," said the whore. "I have an empty room up the stairs right now. How about you, handsome man? Do you want to experience my pleasures?"

Martine almost screamed out when she saw the whore going after her father.

"These men are not interested, Cinnamon," said David, pulling the girl away from Madoc, even though Madoc wasn't interested or responding to her at all.

"Of course, they are," said Cinnamon, setting her sights on Lord Corbett next. "Any man away at battle for so long has got to have a little longing for the flesh of a supple woman."

"This is going badly." Martine closed the door and walked back into the kitchen, pacing back and forth. "I've got to do something quickly. I've got to help out poor David."

"Give me that!" screamed Farley. The sound of his cleaver smashing into the table and the dog's paws slipping on the floor took Martine's attention. She looked over to see Patch running away from Farley with a sausage hanging out of his mouth.

"Don't you dare hurt Patch!" She hunkered down and the dog ran up to her with the sausage still sticking out of his mouth.

"That's meat for the nobles," yelled Farley. "Give it back to me." He yanked his cleaver out of the wooden table and stormed across the room toward the dog.

"Farley, leave the poor dog be," commanded Martine, standing in front of the hound with her arms out to the sides. "He's hungry. Just let him eat the sausage."

"Then your precious nobles will have pottage made from only vegetables, my lady," snarled Farley.

"Then so be it." She pet Patch on the head again as the dog devoured the stolen sausage.

"Where is Matilda? The bread is burning and I need to get it off the fire and this food is getting cold," complained Greta.

"I'll take the tray, Mother." Cecelia threw down the rag and took a step but stopped and rubbed her belly.

"Nay. We don't need another early birth," said Martine. Without a second thought, she snatched up the tray of food, balancing it with her shoulder. "Open the door for me, Greta."

"My lady, what are you doing?" gasped the woman, running to get the door.

"If I'm going to be the wife of an innkeeper, then I need to do whatever is expected of me."

Martine entered the tavern feeling so nervous that she wasn't sure she wouldn't end up swooning once again.

. . .

David had a hard time pulling Cinnamon away from the nobles, because she didn't want to go. He still held the bottle of whisky in one hand, but grabbed the whore's wrist with his other hand.

"Get upstairs and stay there," he ground out, so only she could hear.

"I'm not going to make a penny tonight with these nobles here," spat Cinnamon. "I need money to live on. You can't take away my business like this, David."

"Go!" he ordered, and Cinnamon slinked off to the drink board instead of heading up the stairs. He saw Ava standing nearby and glared at her, sending her sprinting up the stairs to her room. Her brother, Oldrich, still manned the door with David's blind uncle.

David was about to try befriending the nobles once again when the kitchen door opened and Patch ran out, followed by Martine dressed like a commoner and carrying a tray of food.

"Oh, hell, no," he groaned, not knowing how to stop her. This was going to be disastrous. Why hadn't she stayed in the kitchen like he'd told her to do?

"Oh, good. Here comes our food," said Rook, looking up and making a face when he saw Martine.

"What's the matter?" asked Robin, taking a drink. His gaze followed Rook's and he spat a stream of whisky across the table, hitting Gar on the chest.

"What the hell," mumbled Gar. "I've got my own Mountain Magic, Robin, but thank you for sharing yours just the same."

"Martine?" Robin slowly put down his cup and stood. "What in the devil's name are you doing dressed like that?"

"And carrying that tray?" asked her father. "Is this some kind of bad jest?"

"What's going on here?" asked Corbett.

"Stop that, Sister. Put that down right now," commanded Robin.

"Nay, Robin. I'm helping out the Stone family since they were kind enough to aid your wife when she had her baby early."

"This is insane," said Madoc.

"Nay, it's not." She slid the huge tray of food onto the table and started to remove the bowls and hand them to the nobles, one by one.

"I've got it, Martine." David ran over to her and took over serving the food.

"Did you just call my daughter, Martine, without having the respect to use her title?" asked Madoc, standing up like Robin and looking as if he were going to punch David.

"I– I– I am sorry, my lord," stuttered David.

"Rook, help me," Martine whispered to her cousin.

"Sure," said Rook, taking a bowl of food off the tray and putting it in front of himself.

"Not with the food," she said through her teeth. "You know what I mean."

"What does she mean?" asked Madoc. "I'd really like to know what is going on here."

"Nothing out of the ordinary for our family," said Rook, picking up a spoon and scooping food into his mouth. "Mmm, this is good. Did you make it, Martine?"

"Of course, she didn't, she's a noble," snapped her father. Then he looked up to Martine and seemed to cringe. "Did you?" he wanted to know.

"I helped, but I cannot take all the credit." Martine smiled at the men but they were all frowning at her. Even David. "David, I think we'd better tell them."

"Tell us what?" asked Lord Gar.

"I'll tell you," said Rook, ripping off a hunk of bread. "Martine is the owner of the Cross Hare Inn now, that's why she's doing this menial task."

"Owner?" asked Robin.

"Does this have something to do with the fact that the Stone family is four months behind in their rent?" asked Corbett.

"Yes, it does," said Martine. "I was helping Raven collect the rents while you were away, Lord Corbett."

"You did what? Why?" Her father didn't like that idea either.

"Father, please. I'm trying to explain," said Martine. "Now, will everyone please sit back down?"

She didn't think they would, but finally, Robin sat and the rest followed.

"Have some bread," said Rook, ripping off a piece and handing it to Robin. "It tastes a little like ash, but it's hot. Not bad for brown bread, actually."

"Martine, let me explain. It's the least I can do." David stepped forward and spoke to the table of nobles. "We have been struggling since the death of my father, and sadly we ended up four months late with our rent for some reason, even though the ledgers said we were fine."

"That makes no sense," said Corbett. "You obviously don't know how to balance a ledger."

"Yes, he does, Uncle Corbett," interrupted Martine. "I've

looked at the books myself and David's calculations were correct."

"Why were you even doing that?" asked her father.

"We lost the inn," said David. "But Lady Martine was kind. Instead of having to hand over the business and move out, she took over ownership and let us stay. She said she'd help us earn the money to pay our debts."

"I told him I'd give them back the inn if they could raise the money before you returned, but we had no idea you'd be back so soon," explained Martine.

"Martine, you never should have taken it upon yourself to do such a stupid thing," said her brother.

"On the contrary, my lord, your sister's ideas were brilliant and really worked," said David.

"Brilliant? What does my sister know about running a tavern?" asked Robin.

"Enough to be able to help them earn back most of the money to pay off the overdue rent," said Martine.

"That's right," said David excitedly. "The inn is crowded tonight so I'm sure we'll have the rest of the funds by the end of the night, my lords."

"You are a noble, Martine," said her father. "You shouldn't be helping commoners."

"Neither did they have any obligation to help Sage, yet they did," Martine told him. "Without them, baby Martin and Sage might not be here today."

"I'm sorry," said Robin, shaking his head. "I should be thanking you and your family, David. Please, accept my apology and know that I am grateful for all you and your family have done for my wife and baby while I was away." Robin reached out and shook David's hand.

Clapping went up from the patrons in the tavern, since everyone was watching and listening now.

"Uncle Corbett, are you angry with me for what I did?" asked Martine. "I just couldn't let the Stone family lose their home and business after they'd been so kind to help us in our time of need."

"They really did take us in with open arms," said Gar, sounding remorseful too. "If they hadn't let us use their living quarters, I would have had to carry Sage all the way to the castle in a storm since the wheel was broken on the wagon."

"A wheel that David and his brother fixed during the storm, I might add." Martine looked over and nodded to David.

"I suppose you did a good thing," said Corbett. "However, the rent is still due. I can make no exceptions."

"I might already have enough money," said David, shaking a pouch at his side. "Lord Corbett, let me get my cash box. I want to pay you in full right now."

"All right," said Corbett, sitting back down. The room remained quiet as David hurried over to the drink board and pulled out his key. He slid the key into the lock and pulled out the cash box, bringing it directly to Lord Corbett and handing it to him.

"Here is what we owe. And everything we make tonight will be added to the funds as well." David pushed the box over to Corbett. Corbett slowly opened the lid and anger crossed his face.

"What kind of foolish jest is this?" he spat.

"What's wrong?" asked Martine.

"The box has no coins in it."

"Yes, it does, Lord Corbett. There is enough there to cover more than three month's rent." David rushed over and looked into the box. A shadow washed across his face. He looked up at Martine and slowly shook his head.

"What's wrong, David?" asked Martine.

"He's right," said David, looking like he were about to die. "Someone has stolen all the money. The cash box is empty."

CHAPTER 16

"**E**mpty?" gasped Martine, running to the other side of the table. "That's impossible. I counted the money myself earlier today. What David says is true. There was enough there to cover at least three month's rent, mayhap more."

"Well, it's not there now," said Corbett, looking around at everyone looking at him. "I'm sorry, David Stone, but I have to take your inn from you since you cannot pay your debts."

"Nay!" shouted Martine. "I own the inn, and I won't let you take it."

"Martine," said her father in a low voice. "You had no authority to take over the inn. This is Corbett's land and only he can claim the business since the agreement is broken. Not you."

"You can't just throw them out," said Martine. "There is a thief here and we need to find him."

That caused a ruckus with the rest of the customers.

"I'm not going to be blamed for this." A man got up to leave.

"Me either," said another, running for the door.

"Let's all get out of here while we still can," shouted another man, causing all the customers to panic. Everyone ran for the door, not wanting to be imprisoned or be blamed for the work of a thief.

"David, do something," said Martine, but she knew as well as him that there was nothing they could do at this point. Patch started barking furiously from the stairs.

"My lords, if we can just talk about this, I'm sure we can figure out what happened," said David, barely heard over the rustling crowd and the barking of the hound. "Someone shut that dog up," snapped David, looking as if he were ready to lose his temper.

"Patch never barks," said Dirk from the drink board.

"Nay, he doesn't," said Martine, heading over to the stairs where the dog was still barking. She found Cinnamon sneaking down the stairs with a travel bag over her shoulder. Patch kept barking and growling and actually grabbed the bottom of the whore's gown in his mouth and pulled.

"Let go of me, you filthy mutt." Cinnamon slapped at the dog.

Over Martine's shoulder came David's hand. He grabbed the whore's wrist and yanked her down the stairs.

"Going somewhere?" asked David.

"Yes, I'm leaving. I can't make any money here since Lady Martine showed up so why should I stay? Get this dog off of me."

"Martine, would you mind?" asked David, seeming as if he didn't want to let go of the girl, afraid she might run.

"Good boy, Patch," said Martine, reaching over to the table and picking up a piece of meat from Rook's bowl, giving it to the dog.

"Aw, hell, did you really just do that?" complained Rook, more interested in his food than what was going on around him. Rook pushed the bowl away from him and leaned back on the chair and crossed his arms over his chest.

"Give me your money pouch as well as your travel bag," said David.

"What for?" spat the girl.

"What's going on?" asked Dirk, pushing his way up to David.

"I think we've found our thief." David yanked the travel bag away from Cinnamon, handing it to his cousin. "Look through there, Dirk." Then he reached out and plucked the money pouch from the girl's waistband, throwing it down on the table. "And there is all the money from the cash box, I'll bet."

"You can't prove it," spat Cinnamon. "That is all money I earned."

"She's got some fine things in this bag," said Dirk, rummaging through it. "They look like items from nobles if I'm not mistaken."

"Tokens," said Cinnamon. "Things that the nobles don't need and never missed."

"Look at this." Dirk held up a man's ring.

"Let me see that." David reached out and took the ring from him. "It has the letter R on it."

"R? Robin? Is that your ring?" asked Madoc.

Robin's head snapped up and his eyes opened wide. "Nay. I've never been with the whore, I swear."

"I've seen that before." Martine took it to inspect it. "Rook, isn't this your ring?"

Rook's eyes were closed as he leaned back on the chair. Slowly his eyes opened. "What?" he asked.

"That's Rook's ring, I know it is," said Martine.

"Let me see that." Rook jumped up and snatched the ring away from her.

"Is it yours, Son?" asked Corbett.

By the look on Rook's face there was no denying it.

"I admit to having had a night with the whore, but it was a long time ago. Before I was married to Rose." He stuck the ring back on his finger.

"It was more than one night," said the whore, licking her lips. "And what a time we had."

"Rook! That is awful. How can you have bedded a woman like her?" asked Martine.

"It was before I was married. Tell them, Sin."

"It was," she finally admitted. "And I am only telling them because you were always my favorite customer, Rook."

"What? Why is everyone looking at me?" asked Rook with a shrug, blowing on his ring and cleaning it on his sleeve.

"I still can't believe you bedded a whore," said Martine.

"Well, I'm sure your father and the rest of the nobles can't believe you bedded David," said Cinnamon, glaring at Martine.

"What?" asked Madoc. "Daughter, tell me this isn't so."

Martine looked over to Rook for help but her cousin just shrugged. "She took a risk and it paid off, I guess," mumbled Rook, sitting back down and pulling the bowl of food closer.

"Before anyone says another thing, I'd like to say something," said David.

"Yes, please do." Madoc glared at David, looking like he wanted to kill him.

"I wanted to wait until I had enough proof," said David. "But even without counting the coins, I can tell you that this woman is a thief. I am sure she's been stealing from me ever since my father passed away."

"You can't prove it," said Cinnamon.

"The dog is a good judge of character," Martine pointed out. "He knew you were guilty."

"You can't go by that," said the whore. "It proves nothing."

"Let me through. Out of the way." Joe used his walking cane to tap the floor, making his way to the front of the crowd. "I can tell you something that might make a difference."

"What is it, Uncle Joe?" asked David.

"I might not have eyes to see, but I have pretty good ears."

"What does that have to do with anything?" asked Cinnamon.

"For a while now, I've heard footsteps on these stairs at night while everyone is sleeping. I've also heard something that sounded like metal and wood creaking, coming from behind the drink board after the business is closed."

"What are you saying? What was it?" asked Dirk.

"I didn't think much of it until now, but now I am sure it was the sound of a key turning in the lock of the secret compartment where David keeps the cash box."

"That's silly. Everyone knows that David is the only one who has a key," said Cinnamon.

"Not true." This came from Rook.

"What are you saying?" asked Corbett.

"About a year ago, I saw Cinnamon in town. She asked me to have another key made. I thought it was for the door to her room because that's what she told me. She said she wanted to give it to a client to come and go as he pleased."

"Rook, don't tell them," said the girl.

"You helped her to make another key for my cash box?" asked David.

"Not knowingly." Rook shrugged. "If I had known her intentions, I never would have helped her."

"That's a lie. I did no such thing." The whore still denied everything.

"Really." Rook walked up to the whore and reached for her cleavage. He plucked a key out from between her breasts and handed it to David. "Look familiar?"

"It's exactly the same," said David, holding the keys together.

"How did you know she'd have it, there?" Robin wanted to know.

"That's where she always keeps her valuables," said Rook.

"So you really have been stealing from me since my father died?" David asked the girl.

"I had to do something to survive when you started changing all the rules. Especially when *she* showed up and made me give up half my earnings." Cinnamon jerked her head at Martine.

"You disgust me," said David, his eyes still on the keys in

his hand. "Because of your greediness, my family nearly lost our business and even a place to live. If it weren't for Martine, we would be homeless right now."

"There you go calling her by her name with no title again," said Madoc. "And what did the whore say about you bedding my daughter?"

"She's a liar and a thief," said Martine. "Father, David has been nothing but a gentleman toward me."

"Martine means everything to me, my lord," said David. "I wanted to get the deed back to my inn before I approached you, but it can no longer wait."

"What can't wait?" asked Madoc.

"I am in love with your daughter."

"What?" gasped Madoc.

"I'm in love with David, too, Father," said Martine, taking David's hand.

"My lord," said David, bowing as he spoke. "If I may be so bold, I'd like to ask for Lady Martine's hand in marriage."

"That is too bold," said Madoc. "Why would I ever let my noble daughter marry an innkeeper?"

"Mayhap because I married a commoner, Father?" asked Robin, looking over at Martine and smiling.

"And me too." Rook winked at Martine.

Gar cleared his throat. "I might have married from below the salt as well."

"Might?" asked Martine. "Don't let Josefina hear you say that."

"All right. I did marry a commoner. There, I said it."

"So did Raven," Rook reminded them all.

"And cousins Eleanor and Lark did too," added Martine.

"All right, enough," said Madoc. "I know how hard this

must be for you, David. I'm not sure if you know it, but I was raised by the wife of a pirate and was a thief before I married my noble wife."

"So I'm not the only thief?" asked Cinnamon with a snort.

"He was doing what he had to do to survive," Madoc's brother, Corbett, came to his aid. "It was only because he didn't know it but he was really a noble, stolen as a baby."

"And I turned out all right," said Madoc with a smile.

"Father, please," said Martine. "David asked you a question."

"Lord Madoc, I love your daughter and will do anything I can to make her happy."

"How happy can she be? You're an innkeeper," said Madoc, still not accepting David.

"I know I don't have much, but I promise to always love her and protect her. I will be the best husband to her that I can."

"Martine? You really want to marry this man and live at an inn?" asked Madoc.

"Well... yes, I want to marry him," she said, her eyes flicking over to David. "As for where we'll live, I haven't had a chance yet to discuss that with David."

"Martine, what are you saying?" asked David.

"I'm not sure I want to live in one room with your family and raise a child in a tavern," Martine told him. "Mayhap we could live at the castle?"

"And what would I do for a living?" asked David. "I'm not a noble."

"You'll be one," said Rook. "As soon as you marry my cousin, you'll get your courtesy title."

"I appreciate it, but I'm not sure that's who I am," said David sadly.

"You fool," said Uncle Joe. "Stones don't give up. They go after what they want. How many times do I need to remind you, boy?"

"Uncle Joe, I want to be with Martine more than anything. It's just that I'm not sure she wants to be with me as much."

Martine felt the walls crumbling down around her. She'd never known anyone like David and she wasn't going to lose him. "I will," said Martine.

"What?" asked David.

"If you want me to work the inn with you and live in one room with the rest of your family, then I'll do it."

"Martine? Are you mad?" asked her brother.

"Yes. I'm madly in love with David," said Martine, taking his hand. She reached up and kissed him on the mouth right there in front of everyone. "I love him and I want him as my husband."

"Even if you have to give up your life at the castle?" asked David.

Martine took a deep breath and released it, nodding. "Yes. I am willing to give up everything, just to be with you, David."

"Nay," he said, shaking his head.

"What?" she asked in surprise.

"I can't let you do that."

"Isn't this touching?" muttered Rook.

"If I agree to let you marry my daughter, it's only if you move to the castle with her," said Madoc.

"Father, don't do that," begged Martine.

"Nay, he's right," said David. "Lord Madoc, I promise to move to the castle if you'll let me marry your daughter."

"You're going to give up the inn then?" asked Martine in shock.

"I'll give it to my family. That is, if Lord Corbett allows it." David looked over to Corbett.

"As long as the rent is paid up, I don't care who sleeps and works here," said Corbett.

"Speaking of that. Where is Cinnamon?" asked David.

The dog started barking and growling again, alerting all of them that the whore was trying to sneak out the front door.

"Let go of my leg you mangy mutt," snapped the whore, trying to slap the dog away.

"If I agree to let you two marry, can we go back to Blake Castle to finish this celebration?" asked Madoc with a smile.

"Does that mean yes, Father?" Martine squeezed David's hand.

"Corbett, you're never going to clear the family name," Madoc told his brother.

"What does that mean?" asked David.

"It means, yes, David Stone," said Madoc. "I give you permission to marry my daughter, Martine."

"Thank you, my lord." David took Madoc's hand and pumped it furiously. "This has made me the happiest man in the world."

"Thank you, Father!" Martine wrapped her arms around her father's chest, giving him a big hug.

"What about the whore?" asked Dirk.

"She needs to be imprisoned for thievery," said Uncle Joe.

Oldrich pulled the dog off of Cinnamon, taking her into his arms. "Please, my lords. I'd like to plea for this woman's life."

"Oldrich?" Ava came down the stairs. "What's going on?"

"Ava, I want to bring Cinnamon home to live with us," said Oldrich.

"The whore?" Ava laughed, but no one joined her. "Oh. You're serious?"

"Yes," said Oldrich. "I think she is misunderstood. It might be good for her to start a new life in a new town."

"I agree," said Cinnamon, obviously just not wanting to go to prison.

"That's not the way this works," stated Corbett. "Because of what she did, she'll either rot in the dungeon, or mayhap end up hanging from a rope to pay for her wicked deeds."

"Nay, please, my lord." Cinnamon dropped to her knees and held her hands as if in prayer. "I will confess to everything and return all that I've stolen if you'll just pardon me and let me leave here with Oldrich."

"I don't want her living with us," said Ava, but no one paid any attention to her.

"It's fitting to see you grovel like a dog," said David. Just as the words left his mouth, Patch started humping the whore's leg.

Rook was the first to burst out in laughter. Soon everyone, even those in the kitchen who had just joined them, were laughing, enjoying the show.

"David," said Lord Corbett. "I'll make sure the deed to

your inn is returned, since I can see now what happened. I know you have the money to pay off your debt."

"Thank you, my lord," said David.

"As for the whore, I'll leave that decision to the Lord Warden since he is the one who hears the trials. Lord Garrett?"

Lord Garrett stood up. "Thank you, Lord Corbett, but in this case, I will leave the decision to David, since he and his family were the ones to suffer."

"Me?" asked David, slapping his hand against his chest. "I'm just a commoner."

"Not for long," Rook said, making them all laugh again.

"Martine, what should I do? What do you think?" David looked to her for his answer. She appreciated the fact he respected her enough to ask her opinion. However, she didn't feel comfortable making this decision.

"You do what you feel is right," she told him. "After all, she did steal from you and almost ruin your business and cause you to lose your home."

"Yes, she did," said David. "Mother, Sisters? Dirk and Uncle Joe? Do you want to see the girl punished?"

"I don't like to see anyone punished," said Greta. Her daughters nodded in agreement.

"I don't know," said Dirk.

"It's up to you," answered Uncle Joe. "We are no longer in danger of losing the inn and she's confessed."

"Yes," said Martine. "She did give back the money."

"But she did something horrible. She's a thief," said David. "Surely, you must think she needs to be punished for it."

"I agree, punish her," Ava spoke up. "Put her in the

dungeon. Kill her! Do anything at all to her, but she is not going home with us."

"Hold on," said David, putting his hand in the air. "I've made my decision."

"What is it?" asked the Lord Warden. "Do you want her imprisoned?"

"Yes, and no," he said.

"David, what on earth does that mean?" asked Martine.

"I, Lord Warden, would like to suggest that Cinnamon goes to live with Oldrich and Ava in Northumbria."

"What? Nay!" spat Ava.

"Thank you," said Cinnamon, but David wasn't done.

"There's more," he said. "Once they are there, Cinnamon must marry Oldrich."

"Thank you," said Oldrich, happy about the decision.

"Marry? Him?" asked Cinnamon, wrinkling her nose.

"What's wrong with marrying my brother?" Ava asked, looking like she wanted a fight.

"I can't be married. Not in my profession."

"That's the last part," said David. "Cinnamon must give up being a whore."

"Give it up? Never," said the whore.

"It's either that, or you go to prison or a convent," David told her.

Rook started chuckling again.

"I'll do it," scowled the whore.

"That sounds more than fair to me," agreed the Lord Warden. "So be it."

"David, that was kind of you, but why did you do that?" whispered Martine.

"I'm not as kind as you think." He smiled and nodded to

the door. Ava and Cinnamon were arguing, their faces almost touching. Oldrich was trying to break them apart.

"Oh, I see," said Martine. "Very clever. Now, they are all imprisoned with each other."

"Exactly," said David, pulling her into his arms and kissing her on the mouth. He heard someone clear their throat and looked up to see all the noblemen staring at them. "Shall I open another bottle of Mountain Magic or did you want to go back to the castle?" asked David.

"No sense wasting all this good food." Rook was the first to sit down and start eating.

"I need a drink," said Madoc, holding out his cup.

"I think we all do," said Corbett, sitting back down at the table.

"Now, we have something else to celebrate," Martine announced to the table. She held up the bottle of whisky. "Let's drink to my marriage to David Stone."

A little too enthused to celebrate the good news, she foolishly took a swig of the Mountain Magic and started coughing. It was so strong that it burned her throat and she struggled to breathe.

"Martine, give me that." David took the bottle from her and pushed a goblet filled with a golden liquid into her hand.

"What is this?" she asked, still coughing.

"Something I know you can handle and that you like," David answered. "It's sweet mead."

"You are the best, David." She raised her goblet while the others raised their cups. And together they celebrated the beginning of a promise of a new life between Martine and David.

CHAPTER 17
A WEEK LATER

B lake Castle had never looked better than now, decorated in pine boughs and lots of colorful ribbons. It was where the wedding of Martine and David was being held. Since it was winter and using the outdoors wasn't a choice, they'd had to have the ceremony and celebration inside. With David's entire family, not to mention all of Martine's siblings, cousins, aunts and uncles there too, it had been too many to ever fit into the tavern. Therefore, the great hall was the only place big enough to hold the event.

After the vows had been said, everyone headed to the tables to partake of the wedding feast. David had been allowed to sit above the salt since he was now a lord in name only. It had felt odd looking at his family down below, but he was Martine's husband now and his life was about to change dramatically.

David and Martine walked hand in hand through the hall, having had more food at this feast than David had ever seen in his life.

"How did you like the meal?" asked Martine.

"It was very filling. And rich."

"Wasn't the peacock spectacular? And I'll bet you've never had venison before."

"The bird was cooked and stuffed and the feathers reattached," said David. "It was amazing. Farley is still trying to figure out how they did it."

Martine giggled, reaching over to hug and kiss David. "I am so happy to be your wife," she told him. "I am glad my father agreed."

"Me too," said David, leaning in closer to her. "But I still don't feel good about you lying to him when you said we hadn't made love."

"I didn't say that," she corrected him. "I said you were a perfect gentleman, and believe me you were!"

"Oh. So, we should probably keep the truth to ourselves?"

"Unless you want to face my father when he's angry, I'd say it's a much better idea to keep it quiet. Besides, it no longer matters. We are married now, and tonight we'll make love more than once, I'm certain."

"I can't wait." He pulled her closer and kissed her passionately.

"Martine, I havena had time to congratulate ye." A blonde woman who was pregnant joined them. A man with long dark hair was with her and so was a young girl who looked to be about five or six.

"Thank you, Lark." Martine hugged the girl. "David, this is my cousin, Lady Lark, her husband, Lord Dustin, and their daughter, Florie."

"Hello," said David, greeting them all.

"My da used to be my tutor," said the child.

"Really?" David took interest in this. "So, you have a courtesy title too?" asked David.

"I do," said Dustin, pulling his wife closer. "We're also having a baby," he said.

"Congratulations," David answered.

"Och, here come Raven and Sage and the baby," said Lark. "Raven, I hear ye have been feelin' quite ill with yer pregnancy."

"Not anymore, she's not," said Sage, holding her newborn, Martin.

"I'm feeling much better now that Sage gave me an herbal potion that helps. I almost feel like going out and practicing with my sword," said Raven.

"No swordplay while you're pregnant, sweetheart." Raven's husband, Jonathon, who David met earlier walked up with Sage's husband, Robin.

"Jonathon, if we have a boy will you make him a sword in the forge?" asked Raven.

"I'll make a sword if it's a girl or a boy," answered Jonathon. "But only when I think our child is ready for one."

"Ah, here you all are." Gar approached with Josefina. "Rook wants us over by the fire."

"What for?" asked Josefina.

"Rose is planning their summer garden and he is tired of hearing about it. Let's go save him," Gar told the men.

"She's planning a garden?" asked Sage. "Oh, Robin, I want a garden too. We can grow lots of herbs so I can teach baby Martin how to make healing potions."

"He's a baby, Sage," grumbled Robin as the group walked away.

"Martine, I'm so happy for you." A red-haired noble-woman approached with a nobleman.

"Eleanor! I am so happy you could make it to our wedding. David, this is my cousin, Lady Eleanor and her husband, Lord Connor."

"So nice to meet you," said David. "Lord Connor, can I ask, is your title a courtesy one as well?"

"Yes, and no," he told him.

"What does that mean?" asked David.

"Connor was a hangman," Martine whispered behind her hand.

"Really?" David's brows rose in surprise. "And I thought a noble marrying an innkeeper was far below them."

"I was a noble first," explained Connor. "Then, I was an executioner for a while, but a noble again. So, as I said, yes and no."

"Connor, you're just going to confuse poor David," said his wife. "Let's leave them be. This is their special day and you can tell him all about it later."

"My dear daughter."

David turned to see Martine's mother, Lady Abigail, with a sweet smile on her face, hugging Martine. Her husband, Lord Madoc was with her, and they both were dressed in fur and velvet, looking so elegant today. With them were David's mother, sisters, cousin and uncle. Martine had made sure his family was dressed just as nicely as hers for the wedding. His mother confessed to him earlier that she enjoyed wearing the gown of a noble, but Dirk complained that he wanted his old and comfortable clothes back.

"We are so happy to welcome you into the family,

David." Lady Abigail hugged him as well and he didn't stop her from doing it. He'd never had so many hugs from anyone as he had this day.

"Are you sure you won't feel too uncomfortable living at the castle, David?" asked Madoc.

"As long as I'm with the lady I love, I am comfortable anywhere," he said, giving Martine's hand a quick squeeze.

"Good answer," said Madoc with a nod.

Lord Corbett arrived with Lady Devon.

"Thank you, once again, Lord Corbett for letting my family keep the inn even though we were still a little short on paying off all the rent," said David.

"He doesn't mind at all." Lady Devon spoke for her husband.

"Actually, I do," said Corbett. "I think I'm going to have to insist that your family leaves the inn after all."

"Nay!" said Martine. "I thought we had a deal."

"Martine, let him finish," said David, knowing ahead of time what Corbett was going to say since Rook couldn't keep a secret for the life of him.

"The inn is too small for your family," said Corbett. "I've been wanting to build a tavern right here in the courtyard of Blake Castle and I think this would be a perfect opportunity to do so."

"What does that mean, Uncle Corbett?" asked Martine.

"Sweetheart, your uncle is saying I don't need to give up being an innkeeper even though I'm now a lord and living at the castle," David told her.

"I still don't understand," said Martine.

"Lord Corbett is taking us all under his wing," spoke up Uncle Joe.

"That's right," said Dirk. "He's building a tavern inside the courtyard of Blake Castle and he's hired all of us to run it."

"He is?"

"Yes, Martine," said David. "He's also going to make attached living quarters that will be much larger than they have now. The tavern is going to be for nobles only."

"You know all this already?" asked Corbett. "How?"

"Rook might have told me." David chuckled.

"We are delighted to be able to live close to David," said his mother.

"And now, mayhap my baby can be raised alongside yours when you have one, David," said his sister.

"I'd like that," said Martine. "I hope I'm pregnant soon."

"Just not too soon," warned her father, and David knew exactly what he meant.

"I think we need to raise a cup in thanks to all these wonderful people and the most beautiful, wonderful wife that I never thought I'd have." David motioned for a serving wench to come over. She held a large tray with cups filled to the top.

"This one is for you, my lady." David picked up the most ornate silver goblet and handed it to his wife. They all lifted their cups and then drank.

"Ah, Mountain Magic," said Madoc. "Just what I needed."

"Mine is wine," said Lady Devon in confusion.

"Yes, I requested wine for the ladies and whisky for the men," explained David.

Patch ran over to them, being followed by one of the

hounds from the castle. The dog barked playfully and the two dogs ran off to play together.

"I think Patch likes it here too," said Uncle Joe.

"Aye," agreed Dirk. "He's got plenty of other dogs around so he won't feel the need to hump a leg again."

"Martine, my beautiful wife, are you enjoying your drink?" David asked her.

"Martine is drinking white wine?" asked her mother. "She doesn't usually like it."

"Nay, Mother, David has given me a special drink," Martine told her mother.

"What is it?" asked Lady Abigail.

"Only the best for the woman I love." David reached out and stroked Martine's cheek, letting his thumb graze over her lips. "It's ***Sweet Mead for Lady Martine***."

FROM THE AUTHOR

As the author, it is bittersweet to see this series come to an end. Being a next generation series, I have been writing about the Blake family from what seems the beginning of time. The first romance I ever wrote nearly thirty years ago, started out with Corbett Blake and **Lord of the Blade**, of my Legacy of the Blade Series.

I love writing about Corbett and his siblings and now all of their children as well. I hope you enjoyed *Sweet Mead for Lady Martine* and will take a moment to leave me a review.

Be sure to read my **Legacy of the Blade Series** where this all started so long ago.

If you've missed the stories leading up to Sweet Mead for Lady Martine, here is a list:
Below the Salt Series:

Picking up the Gauntlet – Book 1 (Lady Raven is the daughter of Corbett and Devon from Lord of the Blade.)

A Rose Among Thorns – Book 2 (Lord Rook is Raven's twin brother.)

Love Letters for Lady Lark – Book 3 (Lark is the daughter of Storm MacKeefe and Wren from Lady Renegade.)

Dancing on Air – Book 4 (Lady Eleanor is the daughter of Garrett Blackmore and Echo from Lady of the Mist.)

Winter Sage – Book 5 (Lord Robin is the son of Madoc (Echo's twin brother) and Abbey from Lord of Illusion.)

Riding out the Storm – Book 6 (Gar is the son of Echo and stepson/nephew of Garrett from Lady of the Mist.)

Sweet Mead for Lady Martine – Book 7 (Lady Martine is the daughter of Madoc and Abbey from Lord of Illusion.)

At the time of writing this, these are all the books slated for the series. Then again, you never know when another one might pop up so keep an eye open.

You can follow me on social media, and learn more about the books I write.

Stop by and visit my **Website**. You can follow me on **Amazon, Bookbub, Goodreads, Facebook** and **Twitter**. I also have a **Private Readers' Group** on Facebook that I invite you to join.

If you would like to stay informed of my new books and also sales, please be sure to subscribe to my **newsletter** by visiting my site at **http://www.elizabethrosenovels.com.**

Thank you,

Elizabeth Rose

Also by Elizabeth Rose

Medieval Series:

Legendary Bastards of the Crown Series

Seasons of Fortitude Series

Secrets of the Heart Series

Legacy of the Blade Series

Daughters of the Dagger Series

MadMan MacKeefe Series

Barons of the Cinque Ports Series

Holiday Knights Series

Highland Chronicles Series

Pirate Lords Series

Highland Outcasts

Medieval/Paranormal Series:

Elemental Magick Series

Greek Myth Fantasy Series

Tangled Tales Series

Portals of Destiny

Contemporary Series:

Tarnished Saints Series

Working Man Series

Western Series:

Cowboys of the Old West Series

And More!

Please visit http://elizabethrosenovels.com

About Elizabeth

Elizabeth Rose is an award-winning, bestselling author of over 100 books and counting. She writes medieval, historical, contemporary, paranormal, and western romance. Her books are available as EBooks, paperbacks, and some audiobooks as well.

Her favorite characters in her works include dark, dangerous and tortured heroes, and feisty, independent heroines who know how to wield a sword. She loves writing 14th century medieval novels, and is well-known for her many series.

Elizabeth loves the outdoors. In the summertime, you can find her in her secret garden with her laptop, swinging in her hammock working on her next book. Elizabeth is a born storyteller and passionate about sharing her works with her readers.

Please be sure to visit her website at **Elizabethrosenovels.com** to read excerpts from any of her novels and get sneak peeks at covers of upcoming books. You can follow her on **Twitter, Facebook**, **Goodreads** or **BookBub.** Join Elizabeth's **newsletter** so you don't miss out on new releases or upcoming events.

www.ingramcontent.com/pod-product-compliance
Lightning Source LLC
Chambersburg PA
CBHW020133120726
47903CB00007B/2239